'No one – absolutely no one – captures the lovable flaws of the pubescent human creature like Susin Nielsen' *Globe and Mail*

'Unputdownable' *INIS*

Praise for *The Reluctant Journal of Henry K. Larsen*

Winner of the Governor General's Literary Award and the Canadian Library Association's Children's Book of the Year

'A realistic, poignant portrait of one teen who overcomes nearly unbearable feelings of grief and guilt' *Kirkus*

'A fantastic narrator, authentic and endearing . . . a memorable read for all the right reasons' *Booktrust*

'Nielsen writes about the heaviest subjects with the lightest of touches . . . a truly uplifting, even happy read' *Lovereading*

'Gloriously character driven . . . poignant and witty' *Bookbag*

Praise for *Word Nerd*

'Ingenious and warm-hearted, Nielsen's writing boasts believable, unpredictable characterisation' *Guardian*

'Ambrose Bukowski is the titular nerd and it's in his delightful, disarming voice that *Word Nerd* unfolds . . . a funny, wry tale' *Globe and Mail*

'Tender, often funny. It will appeal to word nerds, but even more to anyone who has ever longed for acceptance' *School Library Journal,* starred review

OPTIMISTS DIE FIRST

A NOVEL BY SUSIN NIELSEN

Andersen Press • London

First published in Great Britain in 2017 by
Andersen Press Limited
20 Vauxhall Bridge Road
London SW1V 2SA
www.andersenpress.co.uk

2 4 6 8 10 9 7 5 3 1

British Library Cataloguing in Publication Data available.

Hardback ISBN 978 1 78344 507 3
Trade paperback ISBN 978 1 78344 558 5

Typeset in Garamond Premier Pro by
Palimpsest Book Production Ltd, Falkirk, Stirlingshire

Printed and bound in Great Britain by Clays Limited, Bungay, Suffolk, NR35 1ED

To all the other crazy cat people.
You know who you are.

ONE

The first time I saw the Bionic Man I was covered in sparkles.

It was a typical Friday afternoon at Youth Art Therapy, YART for short. I was trying to help Ivan the Terrible with our latest, lamest project. As per usual, Ivan refused to focus. Instead he tipped a tube of rainbow glitter onto my head, all over my cat hat and all over me. Alonzo tutted sympathetically. Koula snorted with laughter. Another sunny day in paradise.

We were sitting in the common area of the counselling suite. It was always either Antarctica cold or Saudi Arabia hot. Even though it was early January, I'd stripped down to my tie-dyed tank top. Ivan started punching my bare arm with the very fingers that had, moments ago, been wedged up his nose. I reached into my tote bag for my bottle of hand sanitiser, just as one of the counsellors' doors opened.

Ivan glanced up. 'Petula, look,' he said. 'A giant.'

The Bionic Man was not a giant. But he was well over six feet. Everything about him was supersized. A bright orange parka was slung over one arm, which was major overkill for a Vancouver winter. He looked about my age, with a mass of curly brown hair and big brown eyes that were red from crying.

The Bionic Man had stepped out of Carol Polachuk's office. I'd sat in that soulless space many times myself, forced to talk to she of the UP WITH LIFE! T-shirts, bulgy eyes, and condescending attitude. Carol was very good at one thing, and that was making you feel worse. So I wasn't surprised that the Bionic Man looked disorientated. And angry. And deeply, terribly sad.

I recognised those looks. The Bionic Man hadn't been in there for a chat about career options. You didn't see Carol Polachuk for the small stuff. He was one of us.

For a brief moment, our eyes locked.

Then he made a beeline for the doors.

And he immediately left my brainpan as I started slathering myself in hand sanitiser.

The end.

Except it wasn't.

TWO

On Monday afternoon I saw him again.

I stood at the front of history class in my presentation outfit: plain white top with purple crocheted vest, my favourite peasant skirt, and purple rubber boots that hid my lucky striped socks. I was midway through my talk. The assignment: discuss a historical event that has ripple effects to this day.

I'd chosen September 11, 2001. Nine-eleven, the day two planes, hijacked by terrorists, flew into the north and south towers of the World Trade Center in New York City. I meant to talk about the political aftermath, and the many ways it changed how we view personal safety.

But I never made it that far.

A lot of people on the floors below the point of impact were able to escape down stairwells before the towers fell. But the people above the impact must have understood that they were doomed, that no one was coming to rescue them because, well, how could they? Those towers practically rose into the stratosphere.

I thought about those people a lot. How their days started out so normal. How they were average, regular humans; just like me, just like Mom and Dad, just like anyone. I pictured a guy wondering if it was too early to dig into his lunch, because even though it was only just past nine, he was already hungry. I imagined a woman who couldn't stop worrying about her son because he'd cried that morning when she dropped him off at day care.

They were expecting a day like any other.

That part of my presentation was supposed to be brief, just laying out the facts so I could get to the ripple effects.

But I could not shake the thought of all the innocent victims. Or the people they left behind, the children, spouses, parents, and friends whose loved ones were not coming home from work that day, or any day. Their lives from that moment forward would never be the same.

My heart started to race. My breath came in short bursts. I opened my mouth but no words came out. My classmates looked alarmed.

That's when I spotted him, sitting at a desk in the back corner.

The last thought I had was *Oh God I'm wearing my old granny pants oh God please don't let my skirt ride up*—

Then all five feet eleven inches of me crumpled to the floor.

An hour later I was sitting across from Mr Watley in my favourite chair, the one with the nubby multicoloured fabric. I'd sat in it so often in the past two years, its grooves had moulded perfectly to my bum.

It was my favourite because it was the farthest from his bookshelves, which were not secured to the wall in any way. Believe me, I'd checked. So if there was an earthquake – and in Vancouver they say it's a matter of *when,* not *if* – I could be badly injured by falling hard-covers. (I tried not to think about the building itself, which would collapse like a pile of Jenga blocks in any quake over five point zero on the Richter scale. If I thought about that, I would have to leave school, and Vancouver, and live alone in a cave somewhere, which would crush my parents. Plus I would be a sitting duck for any psychopathic serial killer who happened past. And/or I would contract a respiratory illness because of the damp and die a slow, painful death. At least death by earthquake was more likely to be instantaneous.)

In spite of the bookshelves, I liked being in the principal's office. It was a surprisingly warm and cosy space, lit by floor lamps instead of overhead fluorescents. And Mr Watley still had the mason jar snow globe that I'd made for him in the ninth grade on his desk. I picked it up and gave it a good shake, and snow cascaded down onto a little Lego building, which had PRINCESS MARGARET SECONDARY written on it.

Mr Watley gazed at me with his big, watery eyes. He looked a lot like a Saint Bernard. 'Feeling better, Petula?'

'Much. The school nurse gave me a good once-over. Deemed me fit for release.'

'You've been making progress. I was hoping we'd moved past these episodes.'

'Me too.' My last full-blown panic attack had been at least three months earlier, in biology. The topic was infectious diseases. I'd talked about the Ebola virus, which is transmitted through bodily fluids and leads to a truly horrible death. I'd crumpled when I mentioned how easily it could become a worldwide plague.

'At least they're fewer and farther between,' Mr Watley said. He smoothed his hair. I wished his wife would tell him that his comb-over fooled no one. Then again, I'd studied the family photo that sat beside my snow globe many times. It showed a grinning Mr and Mrs Watley and their pug. The dog was far and away the most attractive thing in the picture. My theory was that they had a reciprocal arrangement: Mrs Watley ignored Mr Watley's comb-over, and he ignored the giant mole on her chin. 'Nonetheless, Petula, we've talked about trying to stay away from trigger topics.'

'Yes.'

'You didn't need to talk about the victims at all.'

I glanced out his window at the rain coming down in sheets. 'It was just a small part. If I'd been able to finish, I had some valid points.'

He tented his fingers under his chin. 'Like what?'

'Like that nine-eleven was a game changer. Like we now live in a world where another terrorist attack is a constant threat.'

'I thought we were trying to avoid that kind of negative thinking.'

'Sir, this isn't negative. It's *practical*. My point was, nine-eleven taught us that we all need to be more vigilant. Forewarned is forearmed.'

'I understand that the world doesn't always feel safe. But we live in Vancouver. In Canada. It's—'

'Don't say it, sir. Nowhere is safe.'

'OK, even if we disagree on that point, we still need to keep living our lives, don't we? We can't live in constant fear. We can't look up at every plane that passes, wondering if it's been hijacked. We can't look at every single person we pass in the street, wondering if they're carrying a dirty bomb.'

I can, I thought. *I can be on high alert for the rest of you ignoramuses.* 'No, but it doesn't mean we should bury our heads in the sand. Metaphorically speaking, of course. If you actually buried your head in the sand you would suffocate.'

Mr Watley thought for a moment. Then he pointed at a mug on his desk. 'Look at that and tell me what you see.'

'A half-empty mug of coffee.'

'I see a *half-full* mug of coffee.' He smiled triumphantly, like he'd just said something profound.

'And that's why you'll die before I do.'

He blinked a few times. 'Well, I hope so. I'm fifty-two, after all, and you're only fifteen—'

'Sixteen as of last week. But age aside, studies show that in general, optimists die ten years earlier than pessimists.'

'I find that hard to believe.'

'Of course you do, you're an optimist. You have a

misguided belief that things will go your way. You don't see the dangers till it's too late. Pessimists are more realistic. They take more precautions.'

'That seems like a sad way to govern your life.'

'It's a safe way to govern your life.'

Mr Watley exhaled. He rubbed his watery eyes.

'That's a sure-fire way to get pinkeye.'

He lowered his hand and gazed at me, his expression full of sympathy, which I half hated and half appreciated. 'How's YART going?'

'You know how I feel about that.'

'Yes, and I keep hoping you'll change your mind.' He glanced at the clock. 'OK. Go back to class.'

With only ten minutes left till dismissal I had no intention of going back to class. 'Sure thing.' I stood up and gave a little bow in lieu of a germ-sharing handshake.

I walked out of Mr Watley's office, turned left—

And ploughed right into the Bionic Man.

THREE

Textbooks and papers, mine and his, went flying. We both bent down to collect our scattered things and our foreheads connected with a *crack*.

I straightened, rubbing my temple. 'Ow! Jerk!'

'Um, you do know you ran into *me*, right?'

I looked up.

Emphasis on *up*.

See, when you are a young woman of almost Amazonian proportions, looking up at someone is a rare occurrence. But the Bionic Man had at least four inches on me.

I stared for a little too long at his face. His features were just a bit off. Like, if you moved his nose and his eyes a millimetre here and a millimetre there, he'd be almost handsome. Instead he looked like a Picasso, before Pablo went one hundred per cent abstract.

'How are you feeling?' he asked.

I didn't know whether he was referring to our accidental head-butt or to my fainting spell in history class, and I didn't care. I slipped past him and headed to my locker. Post-Maxine, idle chitchat was difficult for me. Also, I had only five minutes left to clear out before the hall filled with students. Last year, when I was worse, I'd seriously considered wearing one of those masks to school, like the ones people wear in China when the pollution gets bad. Now I just did the common-sense basics, like not touching people or surfaces and washing my hands for the length of two rounds of 'Happy Birthday'. And I didn't linger in this hothouse of germs.

The Bionic Man followed me and stood there as I twirled my lock right, then left. 'You shouldn't follow people,' I said. 'Especially girls. It's creepy.' His off-white fisherman's sweater reeked of mothballs.

'Seriously. Are you OK? You dropped like a sack of potatoes.'

Like I needed to be reminded. When I'd come to, Ms Cassan's cardigan was under my head and the Girl Formerly Known as My Best Friend was gazing down at me with concern. 'Did anyone see my underwear?' I blurted.

He looked confused. 'No. Why? Did you want them to?'

'*No.*' I yanked my locker door open and grabbed my pea coat; I was so close to freedom I could almost taste it. But when I tried to step around the Bionic Man, he held out his right hand. 'I should introduce myself. I'm Jacob Cohen.'

I couldn't help it. I gaped.

Because his hand wasn't real. It was sleek, black, and definitely man-made.

He saw me staring at it. 'Pretty cool, huh? Like something out of *I, Robot.*'

'Or *The Iron Giant.*'

'Ha! Yes. Great movie.'

'Better book.' It was one of my childhood favourites.

'It was a book?'

I let that pass. His robot hand still hovered in front of me. 'Go on, shake it,' he said. 'It has twelve different grip patterns.'

I was caught. If I told him the truth – that I never shook hands – he would think his robot limb freaked me out. Which it did. But while my social skills these days were 'subpar', as I'd overheard some girls say in gym class, I wasn't cruel.

So I stuck out my hand. I heard a mechanical whirring sound, and the fingers of his gleaming black fake hand closed over mine. After what felt like an eternity, I heard more whirring and my hand was released.

The bell rang. Anxiety started to rise up in my throat. 'I've really got to go.' I shoved my schoolwork into my tote bag.

'I feel like I've seen you somewhere else. Like, before today. But I only moved here a week ago.'

I clicked my lock into place and slipped past him, down the hall. I wasn't about to tell him where he'd seen me, for his sake and for mine. What happens in counselling services stays in counselling services.

I pushed open the front doors with my elbows and stepped outside. I breathed in, enjoying a moment of temporary relief. I'd survived another school day.

Now I had to survive the journey home.

FOUR

The walk took fifteen minutes. That was a full eight minutes longer than usual because a building between the school and our apartment had been torn down in December, and now a construction site filled almost an entire city block. I had to take a detour to avoid it.

Up ahead, I watched as the Girl Formerly Known as My Best Friend and her posse walked right past the site. I almost shouted out a warning. But I knew she would give me an exasperated, pitying look, so I said nothing. I turned left instead of going straight and ran through my mental checklist.

Cross only at designated crosswalks and intersections, check.

Step into the road only after all vehicular traffic has come to a full stop, check.

Scan pavement for suspicious objects, bags, or parcels, check.

Give wide berth to irresponsible dog owners who don't have said pet on leash even though it's the law, check. Don't become an animal's chew toy, check.

Look over shoulder occasionally to make sure you are not being followed, check.

Rape whistle around neck, check. Keys secured between your knuckles, check.

My knot of anxiety loosened when I arrived on our street, a quiet one-way in Vancouver's West End.

It is a nice street. Chestnut trees line both sides of the road, and the buildings are all low-rise. Ours stands right in the middle of the block, four storeys with a yellow brick exterior, the word ARCADIA over its front door. We're on the top floor, or, as Dad liked to joke, the penthouse.

Our street and our building were not without danger. But I had safe zones, and this was one of them. For one thing, I'd done due diligence when we first moved in over a year ago. I'd anonymously called in all sorts of building inspectors. Thanks to me the wiring is now to code and every apartment has a new sprinkler system. You'd think the absentee landlord would have been pleased, but instead he sent all the tenants a letter, threatening to 'uncover the rat.'

He never did.

He did get one response to his letter, though. A post-card with no return address and a simple message on the back: *Whatever! And you're welcome!*

First thing I did when I entered our apartment was the smell check. On a scale of one to ten, today was a three. Changing the litter in the boxes could wait another day.

Mom's red rubber boots were in the foyer. I put my purple ones beside hers and wriggled out of my pea coat. Anne of Green Gables, Stuart Little, Moominmamma, and Ferdinand crowded around me. 'I'm home,' I called out.

'Hi, Tula. I'm in the bedroom.'

The cats meowed and rubbed against my legs. 'All right, all right, give me a minute,' I said as sternly as I could, which was next to impossible thanks to their dangerous levels of cuteness. I couldn't even get very mad when I dropped my tote bag in the living room and saw that one of them – I'd bet good money it was Anne of Green Gables – had left a shockingly large turd in the middle of the carpet. *How could something so big come out of something so small?* I wondered, not for the first time.

I donned rubber gloves and cleaned up the mess, and checked the phone for messages, hoping I'd beat Mom to it. Sure enough, there was one from the school nurse. I deleted it. Then I got a bag of cat treats from the kitchen and gave the cats two each. 'That'll tide you over till dinner.'

I headed to my parents' bedroom, carrying Ferdinand, the oldest of our cats, in my arms like a furry orange toddler. Mom was at her computer, tapping out an email, still in her work clothes. Her wavy chestnut hair was pulled into a bun. Maxine had had the same light curl to her hair and I'd always felt a bit envious. My hair is boring and straight. I'd cut it short a month earlier, trying to go for the Lena Dunham look. I got Beaker from the Muppets instead.

'Hey, Mom. How was your day?'

'Oh, fine. I sold more books than candles, and that's always a plus.' Mom works for a chain bookstore at a mall in Burnaby, and the managers love her because unlike some of their employees, my mom actually reads.

She sent the email and swivelled in her chair.

My face fell. 'You didn't.' Curled up in her lap were two jet-black cats.

She gave me a look that managed to be sheepish and unapologetic at the same time. 'I did.'

'You promised.'

'I know, I know, but what could I do? Angie called me in a pinch.' Angie runs the Vancouver Feline Rescue Association, where Mom volunteers. 'They found these two abandoned and half-starved under a porch. All the other foster homes are full. Angie dropped them off an hour ago. It's just until we can find them "for ever homes".'

'That's what you said about Anne of Green Gables, Stuart Little, and Moominmamma.'

'It's harder to find homes for the older ones. These two are still young, so it shouldn't be too bad.' Mom held one of the black cats out to me. Ferdinand hissed. 'I'm calling this one Stanley, from *Stanley's Party*. And this one is Alice, from *Alice, I Think*.'

I am a sucker for a feline face. I scratched Stanley's ears and he purred and purred; he seemed good-natured and docile. But it didn't take away from certain cold, hard facts, like the fact that we could barely afford the four cats we already had. 'Dad's going to kill you.'

'I'll deal with Dad,' she said breezily. Like it was going to be the easiest thing on earth.

Mom whipped us up a tofu stir-fry for dinner. I made us a salad from a head of lettuce, peeling off the outer leaves and discarding them, then washing the remaining leaves with a little dish soap. Mom swore she could taste it, but I reminded her that a hint of Joy was better than getting infected with *E. coli*. After we'd served ourselves, I dished out a plate for Dad, pushing his food into a smiley face before covering it with plastic wrap and putting it in the fridge.

We watched cat videos on Mom's laptop while we ate. All six cats hung out in the living room with us. Ferdinand let Stanley and Alice know who was boss. At one point, Alice pawed tentatively at my skirt, then curled up in my lap and fell asleep. Mom smiled. 'You have to admit, it's nice having some new babies.'

Yes, my mom calls the cats her babies. And yes, it's pretty easy to find deeper meaning behind it. But the cats – especially Ferdinand – helped drag her out of her pit of despair after Maxine died, which was something no one else – not me, not my dad, not her therapist – had been able to do.

On the screen, Maru the Japanese cat was trying to fit into boxes that got progressively smaller. I'd seen the video before, but it made me laugh every time.

'Remember when your grandparents sent Maxine that toy stove?' Mom said. 'And she was so much more interested in the box?'

'I helped her make a playhouse out of it.'

'She loved that box.' Mom brought up memories of

my baby sister like this all the time. Sometimes I didn't mind; sometimes I wished she would just shut up.

Tonight I wished she would just shut up.

After I'd loaded the dishwasher and scrubbed the counters with antibacterial cleanser, I took a shower, making sure the rubber mat was secure. The statistics on injuries and deaths due to bathtub falls are eye-popping.

When I was done, I was grateful that the mirror was fogged up so I didn't have to see my tall, scrawny bod naked. 'You have supermodel height without supermodel looks,' a boy named Carl had explained matter-of-factly to me in sixth grade, when I'd had my first of many growth spurts and loomed over the other kids. 'Well, except for your boobs. They're supermodel boobs. Itsy-bitsy.' I was not sad when Carl and his family moved to Moose Jaw, Saskatchewan.

I streaked naked down the hall to my bedroom, tossed my dirty clothes onto the pile on the floor, and put on my penguin onesie. Rachel, the Girl Formerly Known as My Best Friend, had a matching one; we'd made them together, back when we were inseparable. I often wondered if she still wore hers. Once or twice I'd almost emailed her to find out.

Almost.

The tower of books by my bed had been toppled by a feline. After I restacked them, I pulled my scrapbook out from its hiding place under the bed. I had nothing new to add to it, but I glanced through it for a while because it calmed me down.

When I was done I climbed into bed and polished off the latest Ann-Marie MacDonald novel. It's one of the perks of Mom's job; she often gets advance reader's copies of books before they're published, which she passes on to me when she's done.

Just after eleven, I heard Dad come in. A few minutes later, I heard the microwave beeping. I hoped he'd seen the smiley face. I hoped it had made him smile.

I hoped he wouldn't notice Alice and Stanley until morning.

I thought about getting up to join him while he ate. I pictured the two of us sitting on the couch. I pictured putting my feet on his lap. I pictured him joking about the smell before he gave me one of his famous foot massages.

A few years ago – when Maxine was still alive, and life seemed infinite and full of possibility – the Girl Formerly Known as My Best Friend and I had been at her place, making bottle-cap wind chimes. One of the caps had rolled under the TV console. She dug around for it and found not only the cap but also a dusty, caseless DVD called *The Secret*.

'What do you think it is?' she asked.

'Beats me.'

I think we were both afraid to find out. What if her parents were into weird sex? That would be something we could never unknow. But curiosity won out. We popped it into the DVD player.

It wasn't anything to do with sex. It was a kind of self-help video, an instructional guide to happiness through the power of belief. Like, if you cut out a photo of a new car you wanted and stared at the photo all the time and pictured yourself driving the car – if you believed strongly enough that you deserved it – by the sheer power of your belief you would eventually get it. At least, that was my takeaway. Even at twelve and a half we thought it was pretty hokey, but that didn't stop us from trying it for a while. Rachel cut out a picture of all the members of One Direction (because, as she said, 'any of them would do') and tried to imagine that one of them was her boyfriend. I tried something a little more realistic and cut out a photo of a glue gun.

I got the glue gun for Christmas. Rachel didn't get a One Direction boyfriend, but she did briefly go out with a boy who had hair like Niall's.

I wished that by simply picturing me and my dad hanging out on the couch in comfortable silence – maybe even listening to a bit of music – I could make it come true.

But that wasn't how life worked. So I stayed put.

Moominmamma was curled up by my feet. Anne of Green Gables was curled up on my chest.

Maxine used to come into my room at night sometimes and wedge her little body right up against mine. I'd be sticky with sweat by morning, but I never minded, because there was something magnificent about feeling her chubby toddler belly pressing into me, her little chest rising and falling, her hot breath against my cheek.

Before I turned out the light I picked up the photo of my baby sister from my bedside table and kissed it. 'I love you, Maxine. I'm sorry, Maxine.'

I said that every single night.

Because I was the one who'd killed her.

FIVE

I was ten years old when I found out Mom was pregnant with Maxine. We were still living in the apartment on Comox Street. Mom and Dad were forty. They made a point of saying the pregnancy was not an accident but a pleasant surprise.

I was not amused. I had a good life as an only child. But then, in a weirdly awesome bit of synchronicity, Rachel's mom got pregnant, too. The babies were due about three months apart. Rachel and I were crafting fiends, and we realised that the crafting possibilities for newborns were endless. We knitted blueberry caps and made sock monkeys and sewed soft fleece blankets. Suddenly we couldn't wait for our siblings to arrive so we could play dress-up.

Maxine Ella was born first. Because Dad got to choose my first name, Mom got to choose hers, and Maxine was as close as she could get to the name Max, from her favourite children's book, *Where the Wild Things Are*. Dad chose Ella, after Ella Fitzgerald.

Rachel's brother Owen was born shortly afterwards. We were fiercely proud of being big sisters. Yes, we enjoyed dressing them up. But it went much further and deeper than that.

When she wasn't screaming like a banshee, Maxine was the sweetest, happiest little girl. Her favourite book was, no surprise, *Where the Wild Things Are*. She thought it had been written just for her. So, for Maxine's third birthday, Rachel suggested we make her her very own wolf suit.

We picked out a soft, fawn-coloured wool. I knitted the suit and the hood, with its two pointy ears. Rachel sewed a soft fleecy lining. I hand-sewed brown buttons down the front.

Max loved that suit. She wanted to wear it all the time. When Mom or Dad insisted that she take it off, she would drag the suit around, like a blanket. She even slept with it, sucking on the fabric like it was a pacifier.

On November eighteenth, just over two years ago, Mom and Dad went shopping. I stayed home with

Maxine. Rachel was going to come over with Owen, but she called to say he had a fever.

Max was in a rotten mood. She'd woken at five that morning, and by one o'clock she was overtired and miserable. I told her it was time for her nap.

She threw a tantrum. I put her in her room anyway. I could hear her screams from the kitchen, where I was trying to do homework. After a while she calmed down. I walked past her room at one point and heard her talking to herself, playing happily.

Then it got really quiet. I figured she'd fallen asleep.

My parents came home a while later. Dad went into Maxine's room to wake her up.

I still have nightmares about his screams.

Maxine had been using the wolf suit as a blanket. She'd been sucking on one of the buttons, and the button came loose. It lodged in her throat.

She couldn't breathe.

Everyone said it wasn't my fault. Everyone said it was no one's fault; it was just a random, horrible accident.

My head tries to believe it, but my heart can't.

I learned some lessons that day:

1) Life is not fair.
2) Tragedy can strike when you least expect it.

3) Always expect the worst. That way, you might stand a chance of protecting yourself and the ones you love.

SIX

The Bionic Man was in three of my classes.

Three too many, I thought as he sat in front of me in English class on Thursday afternoon, blocking my view. His dark green sweater smelled like sheep.

We were studying *Wuthering Heights,* by Emily Brontë, which had been my and Rachel's favourite book since we were twelve. I'd reread it at least four times.

As the clock crept towards dismissal, Mr Herbert gave us an assignment. 'Instead of a traditional essay, I want you to adapt a portion of the novel – your choice which part. Turn it into a screenplay, a radio play, or a stage play. Or a poem, or the lyrics for a song – whatever you want. The objective is simply to be creative. You'll present your finished work to the class.'

I let out a sigh. Mr Herbert is young for a teacher, and he believes that thinking outside the box – and wearing Converse shoes and Diesel jeans – gives him a dash of cool.

Nope.

'It's due in two weeks,' he continued. 'And to make it a little more fun, you'll be working in pairs.'

No. Nononononononono.

In less than a minute everyone had a partner, including the Girl Formerly Known as My Best Friend. Even Alonzo, my one ray of hope, had paired up.

'All right, anyone without a partner?' asked Mr Herbert.

I slowly raised my hand.

So did the Bionic Man.

He turned around in his seat and grinned. 'Looks like it's you and me, Petunia.'

My skin felt clammy. My heart started pounding. Pairs were for the socially adept. I would have to talk to Mr Watley. Get an exemption, for medical reasons. He could write me a note: *No longer plays well with others.*

When the bell rang I hurried out of class. But Jacob matched my stride. He followed me to my locker. 'So, Petunia—'

'My name is not Petunia! Do I look like a Petunia?'

He gazed at my quilted floral vest and felt flower earrings and I felt the blood rush to my face. 'You really want me to answer that?'

'Who would name their kid *Petunia*? It's *Petula*.'

'No offence, but who would name their kid *Petula*?'

I swivelled my lock. 'My mom and dad tossed a coin. He got to choose my first name and she got to choose my middle. And one of Dad's favourite singers is Petula Clark.' The Bionic Man gave me a blank look. '"Don't Sleep in the Subway"?'

'Oh. Sure. My bubbe loves that song.'

I shot a quick glance at him. He was just this side of good-looking, like one of the lesser Baldwin brothers.

'So what's your middle name?' he asked.

'None of your business.'

'It can't be worse than mine.'

'What's yours?'

'If I tell you, will you tell me?'

'Fine.'

'Schlomo.'

'Really?'

'Really. Your turn.'

'Harriet.'

'Harriet.'

'Yep. After *Harriet the Spy*.'

He made a face. 'I've seen that movie. It wasn't very good.'

'It was a terrible movie! I'm talking about the book.'

'There's a book?'

My mouth dropped open. 'You haven't read *Harriet the Spy*?'

'I'm not much of a reader.'

Good God. '*Harriet the Spy* is only the best kids' book ever written. Louise Fitzhugh gave the world a whole new type of female protagonist. One that was feisty and opinionated and sometimes quite mean.'

'Sounds like you.'

'Please, you don't even know me.'

'I know that you have cats.'

That gave me the creeps. 'How do you know I have cats?'

'Because you are *covered* in cat hair.'

My face burned. Normally I remembered to roll a lint catcher over my clothes before heading to school, but this morning had been crazy. Dad had discovered Alice and Stanley, and as predicted, he'd been furious. I didn't want him or Mom to have anything else to stress about, so I'd fed the cats, scooped their poop, made myself a quick breakfast, packed us all lunch, and tossed in a load of laundry, all before leaving.

I pulled on my pea coat to hide my shame and shoved my cat hat on my head. Then I closed my locker door and scooted around him.

'Hang on. We still need to talk about our assignment.'

I kept going. I pushed open the doors with my elbows and barrelled down the front steps.

Rachel, the Girl Formerly Known as My Best Friend, was huddled with a gaggle of girls in the middle of the walkway.

I froze. *I could join her,* I thought. *I could walk up to her right now. Smile and say hi. One foot in front of the other! Be bold! Be your best self!*

I couldn't do it. I veered to the left, giving the group a wide berth. But those indecisive seconds were all Jacob needed to catch up to me. He had the stride of a giraffe. 'What's up with you and that girl? What's her name, Rachel?'

'Nothing.'

'You stare at her in class all the time.'

'You'd only know that if *you* were staring at *me.*'

'Not really, no. I'm just a keen observer of human behaviour. I have to be if I'm going to be a director.' He waved his flesh-and-bone hand at me. 'For example, I look at you, with your homemade earrings and quilted vest, and I can guess that you're the creative type.'

I allowed myself a minuscule smile.

'And I look at the way you slouch when you walk, like you're ashamed of your height instead of being proud of it and owning it. I see the scowl on your face, which is growing even as I speak, and the way you keep to yourself at school. This leads me to the conclusion that you're a loner. An unhappy, creative loner with a dark side and not a lot of people skills—'

'Shut up!' I yelled, impulsively slugging him in the arm. *'Ow!'*

I'd punched his robot arm. He grabbed it protectively with his other hand. 'Oh, man. I think you broke it. Look. It's not moving.'

'I'm sorry!' Tears pricked my eyes. I'd had some impulse control issues since Maxine's death, but I was trying to work on them. 'I'm so sorry.'

I heard an electronic whir. He extended a bionic finger towards me and grinned. *'E.T. phone home,'* he said. 'I was kidding, Petula. The arm is fine.'

I almost slugged him again. 'You are *such* a jerk!'

'It's made out of carbon fibre. It's super resilient. Watch.' He made a fist with the hand and punched a nearby garbage can. It toppled to the curb. 'See?' He set the can upright. 'Not even a scratch. Makes me feel like Steve Austin.'

'Who?'

'TV series from the seventies. *The Six Million Dollar Man*. But Steve Austin had two bionic legs, one bionic arm, and one bionic eye. I've just got the arm, up to the elbow.'

I made a left turn to avoid going past the construction site. He turned, too. My curiosity got the better of me. 'Can I ask how . . . ?'

'Of course. I was out hiking by myself last year. A boulder came out of nowhere and pinned my arm down. I couldn't move. I kept hoping someone would come by, but day turned to night, night turned to day . . . I thought I was going to die. After a few days I realised I had no choice: if I wanted to live, I was going to have to saw through my own arm with a Swiss Army knife.'

I stared at him. 'Let me guess. You were trapped for one hundred and twenty-seven hours.'

'Yes! How did you know?'

'Because that's the plot of *127 Hours*.'

'Excellent movie. I was pretty happy with how they dealt with my story. And casting James Franco, well –' he indicated himself – 'separated at birth.'

'It wasn't your story. It was Aron Ralston's story. I read the book he wrote.'

'Huh. I didn't know there was a book.'

'Of course you didn't.' I shook my head. 'You are *such* a liar.'

'I prefer the term *storyteller*.'

'Except you're not even telling your own story, you're ripping off someone else's.'

'Again, I prefer the term *homage*.'

We arrived outside the Arcadia. 'This is where I live, so.'

He glanced up the street. 'Hang on. Isn't the school just three blocks that way?'

'Yes.'

'So why did you take a detour?'

I didn't answer. There was no point telling him about the woman killed by a slab of falling concrete in the U.K., or the man run over by a cement mixer in Tennessee, or any of the other freak deaths that had befallen innocent pedestrians as they walked past construction sites.

My head felt itchy, so I pulled off my cat hat. There was still a lot of rainbow glitter stuck in the wool from Ivan's stunt the week before. Little flecks of it floated down, onto my coat and onto the ground.

Jacob's face lost all colour. 'I know where I saw you.'

It was like he'd been pricked with a pin. He deflated. His bravado vanished.

I patted his non-bionic arm with my mittened hand.

'I had that counsellor, too. She's truly awful. So, word of advice: you do not, I repeat *do not,* have to keep seeing her. You have options.'

He didn't answer. He'd gone elsewhere.

I headed up the walk and went inside.

He was still standing on the pavement when I glanced back.

SEVEN

'No.'

'Sorry?'

'You heard me. No.' Mr Watley's arms were crossed over his chest. Thick sprouts of hair poked out from the cuffs of his shirt.

'But I feel I did an excellent job presenting my case.'

'You didn't. And I'm not about to tell a teacher how to run his classroom. Also, and this is at the crux of my decision, it will do you good to work with someone else.'

'It won't.'

'Petula, we've talked about this. You've told me you want to try to reengage with the world—'

'In bite-sized pieces, sir. And not with everyone in the world, and certainly not him.'

Mr Watley tented his fingers under his chin. 'Why not him?'

'Loads of reasons. For one thing, he doesn't read. This speaks of poor moral fibre and probably poor intellect.'

'You're being terribly judgemental. He seems like a decent and smart young man.'

'He's a pain in the bum.'

'That, Petula, is a fine example of the pot calling the kettle black.'

'Sir!'

He stood. 'You have YART in ten minutes. Go.'

'Your lack of civility has been noted,' I said as he shooed me out of his office.

I began my slow walk towards Youth Art Therapy.

The worst part of a bad week.

After Maxine died, my parents insisted I see a grief coun-sellor. But money was tight, and counsellors cost money. So I was sent to see someone at my very own school.

Carol Polachuk told me she specialised in grief counsel-ling, which was a joke because she caused more grief than she cured. I didn't say much in our sessions beyond *yes* and *no*. This bugged the heck out of her and her bulgy eyes.

One day, Carol – exasperated by my silence – said, 'Look, it was an accident. You didn't *mean* to kill your sister.'

She might as well have added, *But you did.*

I only meant to hit the wall behind her when I threw my mug of tea. I didn't mean to clip her on the forehead, or splatter her with the contents. I certainly didn't mean to draw blood. It was a stupid, impulsive move, and I regretted it instantly.

But the way Carol reacted, it was like I'd tried to murder her. She threatened to charge me with assault. My parents were called in. Mr Watley got involved. Meetings took place.

A solution was found. Instead of one-on-one sessions with Carol, I would go once a week to Youth Art Therapy. Everyone at Princess Margaret knows that YART is where truly hopeless sad sacks get sent for an hour a week to *express themselves through art.*

Rachel and I had secretly dubbed it 'Crafting for Crazies.'

In a million years I couldn't have imagined a day where I'd be forced to join their ranks.

'You'll be graded on assignments,' Mr Watley explained to me and my parents. 'It's like a regular art class.'

'Except it isn't,' I said. 'Except I'll be with people who may or may not be criminally insane.'

My parents wouldn't listen. 'This will be a good fit,' Dad said.

'You've always been a passionate crafter,' Mom added.

I tried pointing out the obvious: that I hadn't done any crafting since Maxine died. They said I was being irrational. This would help me get back on my crafting feet.

'How can I get back on my crafting feet if I fear for my life?'

My protests fell on intentionally deaf ears.

I reached the doors to the counselling suite at the same time as Alonzo Perez. Alonzo is beautiful, with dark skin and a slender but muscular frame. He wore hot pink jeans and a formfitting T-shirt that read SLUT. One side of his head was freshly shaved. Of the people in our small band of misfits, I liked Alonzo the best.

Alonzo was in Crafting for Crazies because he tried to kill himself after he came out to his ultra-religious family and they kicked him out of the house. Now he lived with an aunt on the east side.

'Hey, Petula. How are you feeling?' He held the door for me, because he knew I didn't like touching door handles with my bare hands.

'Good, thanks.' Alonzo was in my history class as well as English, so he'd seen me faint.

'Glad to hear it.'

Ivan the Terrible was already sitting at the far end of the table. He's the youngest member of YART, only thirteen, a chubby, sullen kid with black hair and a super-intense, scary gaze. He reminded me of a boy version of Carrie, from one of my favourite Stephen King novels. I wondered if one day he might light the entire counselling suite on fire with his mind.

Ivan also has what our almost-counsellor Betty Ingledrop calls 'periodic outbursts'. Like when he dumped glitter on my head. Or when he chased Alonzo around the room, wielding a mallet. Or when he tried to staple his own thumb to the table.

Ivan's mom drowned two years ago while they were on vacation in Mexico. I tried my best to be nice to him. Partly because I felt bad for him, and partly because I secretly hoped that if he did light the school on fire with his mind, he might let me live.

Alonzo and I sat down. It was Saudi Arabia hot again, so I pulled off my old hand-knit cardigan, just as Koula Apostolos sauntered in.

Koula's a year younger than me and she has the body of an Eastern European shot-put champion: wide, stocky, all muscle. She was wearing a barely-there top with jean shorts over fishnet stockings and a pair of work boots. Her shoulder-length hair was stiff with hair spray.

She once called my sense of fashion the Handmade Granny Look, so I called her sense of fashion the Eighties Slag Look. But I only said it once, because she threatened to punch me if I said it again.

Koula's an alcoholic and a druggie. She was kicked out of Trafalgar Secondary a year ago and transferred here. There were rumours that she'd done something to Carol Polachuk. Something much worse than throwing a mug of tea.

'I've been sober for a month,' she said now, holding up her AA chip as she took a seat.

'Third time lucky?' said Alonzo, because this was the third time since September that Koula had shown us her one-month chip. The last two times she'd gone on a bender to celebrate.

Koula scowled. 'Shut up, you fag.'

'Eat me, you skank.'

Then they started laughing. Alonzo pulled her close and hugged her. I could not begin to understand their friendship.

Betty Ingledrop stepped out of her office, holding a box of mini doughnuts. 'Hi, everyone!' She's young but dresses older. Every week she showcases a different, brightly coloured suit with tan nylons and sensible heels. Today she wore hot pink.

Betty's our art therapist – sort of. She told us when she started that, technically speaking, she wasn't an art therapist *yet;* we were part of her 'clinical practicum'.

'So, you're a student,' Koula said.

'Not exactly. I'm only six months away from getting my diploma.'

'So, you're a student,' said Alonzo.

She'd smiled sweetly at us. 'We're all students in the school of life.'

Betty is nothing if not unflappable.

We also found out that she wanted to work with much younger kids, but this was the only practicum she could get. It went a long way towards explaining her juvenile art projects.

Now, as she approached the table, she swept one arm behind her. 'I'd like you all to welcome a new addition to the group.'

He'd followed her out of her office. He was tall. He had a bionic arm.

He was Jacob.

No. Nonononononononono.

It was my fault. I'd let him know he had options.

He took the seat beside mine. This time he wore a

greyish-white Icelandic sweater, which he started to pull off because of the heat. It took him a while thanks to his bionic hand. Underneath he wore a white T-shirt, which rode up past his belly button till he had a hand free to pull it back down.

Everyone else stared at his bionic arm. I stared at the line of dark hair that ran down into his jeans.

Betty asked us to go around the table and introduce ourselves. Then she said, 'Jacob, would you care to share your story? This is a safe place.'

'Sure.'

We all leaned forward in anticipation, because it's true what they say: misery does love company.

'I was in a plane,' Jacob began, 'flying over the Andes with my rugby team. The plane crashed. Some of us survived, but no one came to our rescue for quite a while. We ran out of food. We had a tough decision to make: starve, or eat our dead friends.'

I shook my head. Alonzo guffawed. But Ivan's eyes were as wide as saucers. 'You mean, like cannibals?'

Jacob nodded.

'What did you do?'

Jacob leaned in close to him. 'I'm here, aren't I?'

Ivan's eyes got even wider.

Koula crossed her arms over her ample chest. 'I call bullshit.'

'Clearly,' said Alonzo.

Jacob grinned. 'Busted. Good movie, though. *Alive*. Directed by Frank Marshall, who also directed the lesser-known *Arachnophobia*.'

'So, you didn't eat human flesh?' asked Ivan.

'No.'

Ivan looked deeply disappointed.

'OK,' said Jacob. 'Here goes. I was sailing with my brother, Buck. A storm came up. Buck died; I lived. Buck was always my mom's favourite—'

'*Ordinary People*,' said Betty, her mouth turned downward.

Jacob nodded, impressed. 'Very good. Won the Oscar for best picture in 1981.'

'Freak,' said Koula.

'Movie freak,' said Jacob.

Our Almost Counsellor cleared her throat. 'Since you're clearly not ready to share, let's move on.' She opened a folder. 'We're going to make origami birds today.' She held up an example. 'Each bird represents an anxiety or fear. You can write the fear on the side of each bird. Then we'll go outside and release them – symbolically cast them away.'

'So, litter,' I said.

'Petula's going to be here all day,' Koula snickered. 'She only has about a jillion and one fears.'

'They're not fears if they're based on research and facts.'

'Says the girl who won't walk past construction sites because she's afraid she'll get killed by falling debris.'

Jacob's thick eyebrows shot up and I knew Thursday's walk was suddenly making sense to him.

'And you reamed me out one day for listening to my iPod on the way to school,' Koula continued.

'You reamed me out about that once, too,' said Alonzo.

My stomach clenched. 'I was merely trying to point out that when you're plugged in like that, you're not aware of your surroundings. You're not going to hear a truck coming, or a rapist—'

'Here, have a doughnut,' Koula interrupted. Her weasel eyes on mine, she stuck her man hand into the box, making sure her fingers touched every single doughnut before she passed the box over.

I stared into the box. 'I'm not hungry.'

Koula laughed. 'Har! Har! Har!' Like a dog's bark. 'Yep. You're going to have to make a whole flock.'

I wanted to punch her.

'Koula,' Betty said. 'Remember our motto: be kind.'

Ivan let rip with a loud toot. 'FYART!'

Fifty minutes later, we all traipsed into the field behind the school, carrying our birds. I'd made six, not because

I needed a flock but because I was good at origami. Alonzo had made a few. Ivan and Koula had made one each. Jacob had made none. 'I can do a lot with this, but origami? Forget it,' he told Betty, indicating his bionic arm.

Betty, ever practical, replied, 'Perhaps Petula would be willing to give you a couple of hers.'

I handed Jacob two birds. He read what I'd written on each. 'Biological warfare. Planes.'

'Told you,' said Koula. 'She's cuckoo for Cocoa Puffs.'

'Actually,' said Betty, 'I'm proud of Petula. *She* took the assignment seriously. *She's* attempting to work on her issues.'

Koula gave Betty the finger when her back was turned.

'All right, everyone, are we ready? Release your fears!'

We tossed the birds into the air.

They pinwheeled straight to the ground.

We stared at them, lying in the mud at our feet.

'In the movie business,' said Jacob, 'we'd call this an anticlimax.'

Minutes later the bell rang and we trudged back to the counselling suite to gather up our things.

'This group,' Jacob said after the others had left. 'It's like a twisted version of *The Breakfast Club*. Koula's like a scarier Ally Sheedy. I'm like a cheerier Judd Nelson.

You're the Molly Ringwald character, only more uptight.' Before I could respond, he took out his phone. 'Can I have your number?'

'Why?'

'So we can book a time to work on our assignment. What's your last name?'

'De Wilde.'

He laughed. I didn't. 'Seriously?'

'It's Belgian. And I don't see what's so funny, Jacob Schlomo Cohen.'

'It's just that you're so *De Not. De Cautious* would have suited you better.' He slipped his sweater back over his head. 'Hey,' he said, his voice muffled by the wool, 'can you help me get this on?'

I saw my out and hurried away.

EIGHT

Maxine visited me in the night. She wanted me to read her *Where the Wild Things Are*. 'The night Max wore her wolf suit,' I began, changing the pronoun. She leaned against me, her thumb in her mouth, hair brushing my cheek. *This is what happiness feels like*, I thought. I breathed her in. She smelled like salt and peaches.

And pancakes. Why pancakes?

I opened my eyes. Ferdinand was on my pillow, inches from my face, purring. I could hear clattering from the kitchen. Suddenly the pancake smell made sense.

Maxine had been gone for two years and three months. In another year she'd be dead longer than she'd been alive. But in my dreams she was still so real. Waking from them

SUSIN NIELSEN

was always a crushing letdown. Like someone had put lead weights on my chest.

Dad poked his head into my room. He was in his ratty terry-cloth bathrobe, a gift from my mom on their first-year anniversary. 'Calling all tall people, breakfast is served!' Dad likes to joke that he and I are 'vertically gifted'. He is six foot four. My mom is a mere five foot five. I land right between the two of them.

I forced myself to smile. 'There in a minute.'

Saturday mornings, my dad is at his best. We don't see much of him during the week because he works a lot, way more than he did when Maxine was alive. But Saturday mornings, he steps up his game. So I forced my sadness inward and climbed out of bed, determined to step up my game, too.

I padded into the kitchen in my penguin onesie. Mom was already at the table, wearing her plaid pyjama bottoms and WHAT WOULD ALICE MUNRO DO? T-shirt. She was drinking a mug of coffee and reading the news on her iPad. Stanley was on her lap. 'Hey, Tula,' she said. I bent down and gave her a hug.

Dad joined us at the table, a plate of pancakes in one hand, a bowl of diced fruit in the other.

'Great pancakes,' I said, digging in.

'Thanks. I put blueberries in them.'

'Maxine loved blueberries,' Mom said. 'Remember she called them *boo-bears*?'

Dad's neck stiffened, so I jumped in.

'How were things at work this week?'

'Good,' he said. 'Busy.'

'Good.'

'And you? School?'

'Good.'

Silence. Dad stood up. 'My feet are cold. Be right back.'

After he'd left the room, Mom said, 'I almost forgot. You'll never guess who I ran into outside the SkyTrain station yesterday.'

'Who?'

'Rachel's mom.'

My stomach lurched.

'She said she wished you girls would try to work things out—'

Dad reappeared in the doorway. When he spoke, his voice was eerily calm. 'There is a turd in my slipper.'

I wish I could say this was a rare occurrence. But Anne of Green Gables is a chronic stealth pooper. If she's unhappy – and a lot of things seem to make her unhappy – she will leave a turd under a cushion, or a blanket, or the couch.

'Just tip it into the toilet and flush it,' said Mom.

I knew this was the wrong answer. Dad's jaw clenched. 'Here you go again. Showing a complete lack of regard for the humans living here—'

'I'll clean it up!' I leapt up from the table. I got rid of the poop and tossed Dad's slippers into the laundry. Then I cleared up and washed all the dishes even though Dad said he could do it, and I vacuumed up all the clumps of cat fur in the living room. I sprayed all surfaces with antibacterial spray and changed the litter boxes. It was part of my strategy: think ahead to things my parents *might* argue about, and try to fix them before they did.

There were days when trying to act like a normal family was exhausting.

When we were around ten years old, Rachel and I went through a Laura Ingalls Wilder phase. We devoured all the books in the *Little House on the Prairie* set. We wished we could be a part of that family. For a while our crafting got seriously farmstead; we stitched a lot of wall samplers and made loads of beeswax candles. And we constantly bugged our parents to take us to Fort Langley so we could see how the pioneers lived.

We even made bonnets. And wore them.

But while I loved Ma and Pa Ingalls, I knew my own parents were pretty cool too. They'd both gotten master's degrees from the University of British Colombia, where they met. Mom's was in children's literature, Dad's in musicology. After they graduated, people weren't exactly beating down the door to hire them. So they took what little savings they had and opened a used bookstore/ record-shop in Kitsilano.

That was the year before I was born, around the time people were starting to order their books online or download them to e-readers, and years after anyone bought records or even owned record players. But Mom searched for first editions, and Dad bought stock at yard sales and flea markets for dirt cheap since so many people were trying to get rid of the stuff he was trying to sell.

For a while, they did OK. They created a niche market for collectors. They saved enough to put a down payment on the Comox Street apartment. My childhood was full of books and music and crafting and laughter, and if you ask me, that is a childhood worth having. 'We aren't rich in money, but we're rich in love,' Mom liked to say.

By the time Mom discovered she was pregnant with Maxine, things had taken a turn. They still had their die-hard customers, but it was harder to compete with online shopping. Then their landlord announced that he'd sold the whole block to a developer. Two years later the mom-and-pop shops were all gone, replaced with condos and chain stores. Dad took a job at an insurance firm. Mom started working at the bookstore in Burnaby. They filled our apartment and storage locker with leftover stock.

But Mom still read to me every night, Dad still played his music all the time, and we danced like goofballs, first the three of us, then the four of us.

Then Maxine died, and Dad stopped playing his records. We sold the apartment on Comox because none of us could stand being there. Scene of the crime and all that.

We moved into the Arcadia. Just the three of us and our invisible zeppelin full of grief.

Maxine's death had shown me that dangers lurk around every corner. So even if my grief and guilt made it hard for me to get out of bed, I knew I needed to do what I could to keep my parents together and safe. And I had to keep myself safe, too, even if I sometimes wished I was dead.

Because I'm it.

I'm the only child my parents have left.

Shortly after breakfast Dad got dressed in his jeans and beloved Nina Simone T-shirt and left for the office. 'A lot of extra paperwork.' As always.

I headed out a while later, shopping list in hand. 'You're taking on all the household chores as a way of doing penance,' Carol Polachuk had said in one of our last sessions, looking pleased with herself. Like I could possibly think that running errands and scrubbing toilets could make up for killing my sister.

It was a rare sunny January day, so I didn't go directly to the supermarket. Instead I took a long walk through the West End. I did a mental count of the transgressions I saw:

4 jaywalkers.

9 cyclists without helmets.

15 people listening to music on headphones, oblivious to their surroundings.

6 people texting while walking, 1 of whom almost got hit by a bus.

8 drivers talking on phones, in spite of the fact that it is AGAINST THE LAW.

2 of said drivers barrelling right through a crosswalk while a pedestrian was waiting to cross.

Either they were stupid, or they were optimists. Most likely both. 'I will outlive you all,' I muttered under my breath.

I walked all the way to Burrard and Georgia, looping around the Vancouver Art Gallery, and heading back along Alberni. Michael's Arts and Crafts was up ahead. I crossed to the other side of the street to avoid it.

That store had been my and Rachel's Mecca. We would spend entire Saturday mornings roaming the aisles, finding materials to make Uglydolls, friendship bracelets, earrings, felt slippers, and Scrabble tile coasters. Then we'd go back to my place or hers and spend all weekend together, crafting, reading, and gossiping.

Now weekends dragged on for ever.

I'd tried to compose an email to her recently. *Dear Rachel: I'm so sorry for everything. I miss you like stink. Please, can we talk?* But I couldn't bring myself to hit Send. I deleted it.

I walked to Lost Lagoon in Stanley Park. It had been one of Maxine's favourite spots. She loved feeding the ducks and sticking her ladybug boots into the shallow water.

A lot of people were out enjoying the sunshine, but I still slipped my keys between my knuckles before I joined the dirt path around the lagoon. I found an empty bench and sat down. I let myself cry. Sometimes the pain was physical, like someone had driven over me with a steamroller and left me flattened like in a cartoon.

After an hour or so I got up and continued along the path. A man was sitting on a bench up ahead. It looked like my dad.

It *was* my dad. He was gazing into the middle distance.

I was pretty sure he'd chosen this spot for the same reason I had.

'Dad. Hi.'

His eyes took a moment to focus. 'Oh. Hi.'

'I thought you were at work.'

'I was. Just thought I'd get in a walk before heading home.'

I moved his briefcase so I could sit beside him. It was surprisingly light, like it was a prop. Like maybe he hadn't been at the office at all.

Instinctively I slipped my mittened hand into his. He squeezed it tight for a moment.

Then he let go.

He never says it. He doesn't have to.

I know he blames me.

Dad helped me shop. We got back to the Arcadia about an hour later. He pushed the button for the elevator. I headed for the stairs. 'You should walk up with me.'

'I've told you before, I'm not enabling your phobias.'

'They are not phobias! Google *elevator deaths*. You'll never get in an elevator again.'

'Which is why I won't Google it.' He took the bags from me as the elevator arrived. I ran up the stairs two at a time, trying to beat him. But he was already opening our apartment door when I emerged from the stairwell, out of breath.

Mom shot into the foyer when she heard us. 'Petula! I was just about to text you.'

'Why?'

She tilted her head towards the living room. 'You have company. The boy you're doing the English assignment with?'

No. Nonononononono.

She added in a whisper, 'He's awfully cute!'

NINE

'So, tell us about this assignment,' Mom said as she handed Jacob a plate of cookies. Her voice was higher-pitched than usual. Overeager. It made me cringe. As did the fact that she was still in her pyjama bottoms and WHAT WOULD ALICE MUNRO DO? T-shirt. Meaning, she hadn't changed. Meaning, she still wasn't wearing a bra.

Jacob wore another sweater; he had quite the collection. This one looked like a Cowichan design, in browns and off-whites, with two bears on the front. He grabbed two cookies with his real hand, just as Anne of Green Gables leapt onto his lap. 'We have to adapt a scene from *Wuthering Heights* into another format,' he said. 'Like a screenplay, or a song.' He started manipulating his bionic arm for the cat.

Mom glanced at his arm but said nothing. '*Wuthering Heights* is one of Petula's favourites.' She looked at me, willing me to join the conversation.

But I couldn't. I was seeing our apartment through Jacob's eyes. Our furniture, a mishmash of antiques that had belonged to my mom's grandparents, took up a lot of floor space. Most of it was worn and tattered, destroyed by years of kids and cat claws. The carpet was strewn with toy mice and tufts of fur, even though I'd vacuumed that morning. Two different cat gyms, plus Dad's records, Mom's books, family photos, and a bunch of my old crafts, meant there was little room left for humans. I stared at my feet. To add insult to injury, there was a hole in my left sock. Not only did my toenails need clipping, there was a hair growing out of the knuckle of my big toe.

Dad joined us from the kitchen, carrying a tray. He passed out tea in mismatched mugs. Of course Jacob had to get the one that read WORLD'S BEST FARTHER. 'It's so nice to meet one of Petula's friends.'

'It really is,' said Mom. 'She never brings friends home these days.'

Thank you, Mom! Thank you so much! Of course I

didn't bring home friends. I didn't have any. And even if I did, I wouldn't have brought them here. I knew how we looked to the outside world. The last 'friend' to visit had been a girl in my grade named Brittany. Mr Watley had asked her to bring me some schoolwork when I'd been home sick. Mom had been fostering a litter of kittens, so we'd had eight cats, an unusually high number. Brittany had told everyone at school that our apartment smelled bad and that we had enough cats to be on an episode of *Animal Hoarders*.

Bitch.

'I like your apartment, Mr and Mrs De Wilde,' Jacob said. 'It's very homey. Lived in.' I was sure he meant it as an insult.

'Please, call us Virginia and Andreas,' said my dad.

'Who's the record collector?'

'Me. It's old stock. We used to own a second-hand book-and-record shop.'

'Wow. Cool.'

'It was cool,' Dad agreed, sipping his tea. 'While it lasted.'

'Jacob, are you new at Princess Margaret?' asked Mom.

He nodded. 'We moved here from Toronto last month. My parents got job transfers.' Alice and Stanley wandered in, followed by Ferdinand. Ferdinand leapt onto my mom's lap. I could see Jacob doing a mental head count. 'How many cats do you have?'

'Currently? Six,' Mom replied. *Shoot me now.* 'I volunteer for the Vancouver Feline Rescue Association. So, four have pretty much become permanently ours, and the other two I'm fostering until we can find them forever homes.'

Dad smiled tightly. 'She's like Mia Farrow or Angelina Jolie, but with cats instead of kids.'

'I wish I could take one,' Jacob said. 'But my mom's allergic.'

'What's your theory, Jacob?' Dad continued. 'Just how many cats does one woman need before she becomes a certified crazy cat lady?'

Mom gave an equally tight smile. 'I prefer to think of myself as a caring human being. Not a concept that's readily understood by some.'

Jacob shifted uncomfortably in his seat and I died a small death. I could just imagine the stories he'd tell at school on Monday.

Dad looked at his watch. 'Oops, got to go. Your mom and I have an appointment at two.' Thank God he didn't mention it was with their marriage counsellor.

They stood up. I turned to Jacob. 'Let's get this over with.' The sooner we got to it, the sooner he would leave.

'You couldn't have called first?' I asked as we entered my room.

'How? You wouldn't give me your number. I had no choice but to come over. Your last name's listed in the building directory.'

I moved to close my door, but he stopped me. 'Leave it open. Please.' I gave him a puzzled look. 'I don't like feeling closed in.'

'You're claustrophobic?'

'Sort of.' He perched on my bed and glanced around my room. 'Wow. You're kind of a pig.'

My face burned. My room is the one place where I feel I can totally let down my guard. I think of it less as *messy* and more as *controlled chaos*. But as I glanced around, I could see Jacob had a point. Dirty clothes were strewn across my floor. My bed, with its colourful homemade quilt and needlepoint throw cushions, was unmade. The cats had tipped over my tower of books, again. My old crafts – a sock monkey, three dream catchers, macramé hangings – were gathering dust. A lone poster – CRAFTERS MAKE BETTER LOVERS – given to me by the Girl Formerly Known as My Best Friend on my thirteenth birthday, was peeling off the wall.

Worst of all, my oldest, saddest pair of granny pants

was lying right near his feet. 'Come sit at my desk.' Once he'd moved, I kicked the pants under my bed.

I powered up my desktop computer, a hand-me-down from my dad. Anne of Green Gables, who had taken a liking to Jacob, wandered in and jumped onto his lap again, kneading her paws into his sweater.

'What kind of adaptation should we do?' I asked.

'How about a screenplay?'

'Any particular scene you want to choose?'

'You pick.'

'Um. Maybe the third chapter?'

'Remind me what happens.'

'Lockwood is reluctantly given a room at Wuthering Heights for the night and the ghost of Catherine comes to the window.'

'It's a ghost story?'

'Not really. I mean, yes, there's a ghost—' I stopped. 'Have you read the book?'

'No.'

'Have you *started* the book?'

'No.'

'Do you read at *all*?'

'To be honest? Not a lot.'

'Oh my God!' I blurted. 'You are such a Cretan!'

His lips curled slightly. 'I believe you mean *cretin*. If I were a Cretan, I'd be from the island of Crete. I may not read a lot, but it doesn't mean I'm an idiot.'

My face felt like it was on fire. *Cretin* was one of those words I'd only seen written down. I'd never heard it said aloud.

'And I do read, just not a lot, and very slowly, because I'm mildly dyslexic. So, you basically just taunted a person with a learning disability. An amputee with a learning disability. Way to be a bully, Petula.' He was clearly enjoying himself.

'I'm sorry,' I muttered. I kept my eyes on the screen so I wouldn't have to look at him. 'Look, why don't I just write the scene and we'll put both our names on it. You don't have to stay.'

'That wouldn't be fair. Why don't you write it, and I'll direct it?'

'Direct what?'

'I think we should make a short. I shot a lot of shorts in Toronto. I've got a great camera.'

'But who would be in it?'

'Some of your friends.'

My silence was his answer.

'How about the people from YART?'

'Please tell me you're joking.'

He ran a hand through his thick hair. 'OK. Why don't

we start by writing the scene, and figure out the rest later? I'll show you how to format.'

It took us about an hour and a half to write the scene. It was mildly fun, writing in screenplay form. I told Jacob the rough plot of the novel as we worked. When we were close to being done he said, 'Can I use your washroom?'

'Just a minute.' I ran down the hall and did a litter box check. I scooped a couple of fresh poops into the toilet, flushed, and spritzed the room with air freshener.

'OK, good to go,' I said when I got back. 'First door on your left.'

But Jacob was no longer at my desk. He was perched on my bed again.

And he was flipping through my scrapbook.

TEN

I marched over and grabbed the scrapbook from his lap. It was open to my most recent page.

Woman Dies from Minor Cut on Finger

A mother of two contracted necrotising fasciitis, more commonly known as flesh-eating disease, after receiving a minor paper cut at work . . .

Child Killed in Roller-Coaster Tragedy

A seven-year-old boy died on Sunday after the safety bar on his roller-coaster car failed to lock properly. Onlookers watched in horror as the boy flew out of the car during the coaster's descent . . .

Man Beheaded in Elevator Accident

Fifty-two-year-old Victor Farmiga was 'a gentleman', say those who knew him. When the elevator in his office building opened its doors slightly above the second floor, he held the doors open and handed the other passengers out. But the elevator suddenly shot upward, beheading Farmiga . . .

Girl, 9, Mauled to Death by Nana's Dogs

Friends and family are reeling after a young girl was attacked by her grandmother's two dogs in the woman's backyard. The girl was rushed to hospital, where she was pronounced dead on arrival . . .

Nurse Killed Walking Past Construction Site

A young nurse was struck and killed by a falling sheet of metal as she walked to her first day on the job at St. Michael's Hospital. Veronica Lamar had just graduated with flying colours from nursing college . . .

Teenager Trampled to Death at Boxing Day Sale

A teenage girl was trampled to death by fellow shoppers looking for a bargain at a popular electronics store on Friday. When the doors opened, the crowds surged forward and the young girl fell to the floor . . .

Child Tumbles Off Balcony Trying to Fly
A three-year-old is dead after she tried to 'fly like Tinker
Bell' from her family's tenth-floor balcony. Her mother is
said to be inconsolable . . .

Man Dies When Basement Swallowed by Sinkhole
A thirty-eight-year-old man was sleeping soundly when a
sinkhole opened up beneath his house, swallowing the lower
floor where his bedroom was located . . .

My breath came in short, sharp bursts. No one, *no one,*
was supposed to see my scrapbook. 'How dare you? How
dare you look through my stuff?' My voice wasn't my
voice. It was screechy.

Jacob didn't even have the decency to look caught. 'I
thought it was a photo album. I didn't know it was page
after page of articles on freak deaths.'

'If you tell anyone—'

'I'm not going to tell anyone. Who would I tell?'

'I don't know! Kids at school? I know people talk about
me. I know people think I'm a weirdo.'

I started to sway, feeling dizzy. 'Whoa,' Jacob said. He
put his hands on my shoulders to steady me. 'Sit,' he said.
Like I was a dog. But I did as I was told. 'Breathe.' I breathed.
'I don't think you're a weirdo. Offbeat, yes. A fatalist, yes.'

'I'm not a fatalist. I'm a pessimist. There's a difference.'

'Why are you a pessimist?'

'It's just common sense. You've heard about Darwin's theory of evolution? Survival of the fittest? The pessimists were the fittest. They were the ones who were wary of neighbouring tribes, or cute little lion cubs. They knew the cute lion cubs' mother was nearby. The optimists were like, "Here, kitty kitty." Their optimism literally killed them.'

'But the optimists were happier, surely.'

'Maybe. But at what cost? Pessimists live longer lives.'

'Smaller lives.'

'Safer lives.'

Jacob indicated the scrapbook. 'This isn't a reflection of reality. You must have to dig deep to uncover these stories.'

'That's the thing, I don't. Tragedies like this happen *every day*. It *is* reality.'

He shook his head, unconvinced. 'OK, but why keep a record?'

I struggled to explain. 'It reminds me to be vigilant. And also . . . it makes me feel like I'm not so alone.' I felt tears sting my eyes. *No. Nonononono. I will not cry in front of him.* I pointed at one of the articles, working hard to steady my voice. 'That grandma. *Her* dogs killed *her* grandchild. How does she live with that? And that mom who let her seven-year-old ride the roller coaster. She'll never forgive herself.'

'It wasn't her fault.'

'Wasn't it? Maybe, if she'd done her research, she wouldn't have let him on that rickety old thing. Maybe he'd still be home, playing with Legos.'

'Have you always seen the world this way?'

'No.'

Jacob took my hand in his real one. It was a big hand, warm and dry, and it encompassed mine. I tried hard not to think about germs. 'What happened to your sister?'

'How do you know I had a sister?'

'Your mom told me.'

Of course she had. Mom couldn't get through a couple of hours without bringing up Maxine.

'She choked to death. On a button. A button I'd sewn onto an outfit I'd made for her, which shouldn't have had buttons in the first place because she was only three.'

'And you think it was your fault.'

'Not think. Know.'

I waited for him to disagree with me, because that's what people did. I waited for him to say, 'That's ridiculous, you're not to blame, blah blah blah.'

But he didn't. 'I get it. I live with that, too.'

I stayed very still.

'My two best friends died. I didn't. Same accident, but I'm still here. Like Harry Potter: the boy who lived.'

'Tell me what happened. The truth this time.'

He looked straight ahead, still holding my hand. 'We had a basketball game, pre-season, north of Toronto. I'm a terrible player. I was only on the team because of my height. I sat on the bench most of the time, but I never cared because my best friends were on the team, too. Randle McMurphy and Ben Willard. The three of us took film studies together and shot shorts all the time. I'd direct and Randle and Ben would write, act, crew – everything.

'Ben was older than us, and he'd just got his full licence. We took his mom's car to the game. Afterwards, we headed back to the city. It was snowing. Dark. A drunk driver. . .'

'No.'

'When I came to, I was pinned under a bunch of crushed metal. The paramedics used the Jaws of Life to get me out. I lost part of my arm. Randle and Ben . . .' His face clouded over. 'Hard not to feel guilty when you're the sole survivor.'

I got it. I was close friends with guilt, and I knew it was seldom rational.

'So here I am. Almost eighteen and repeating eleventh

grade because I flamed out spectacularly last year. It's why we moved here. I just couldn't be in that school any more.'

I squeezed his hand. He grabbed the box of Kleenex I kept by my bed and blew his nose loudly, honking like a Canada goose. Then he tried to hand the tissue to me.

'Um, ew.' I pointed to the garbage can under my desk. He left shortly afterwards.

This time, we exchanged phone numbers.

ELEVEN

By two a.m. I was still wide awake. This happens some-times. I don't like it one bit. Being a loner is entirely different from that middle-of-the-night feeling of being utterly alone.

It's even worse early on a Sunday morning. I hate Sundays, and I'm pretty sure my parents hate them, too. Too much time to spend in our own heads. Too much time to spend together.

I turned on my bedside lamp and reread a chunk of *Wise Blood,* another all-time favourite of mine. Then I got up and turned on my computer. I searched for articles for my scrapbook and printed a few. I watched some of my favourite cat videos.

I was midway through *Henri, the Existential Cat* when an idea struck me.

It was either utterly inspired, or utterly dumb.

I texted Jacob.

What if our 'Wuthering Heights' video didn't star humans?

What if it starred cats?

I didn't expect an answer till morning. But maybe Jacob had his own sleep issues, because a moment later my phone dinged.

I love it.

We texted back and forth to firm up plans.

And for a while, anyway, I didn't feel so alone.

TWELVE

Jacob showed up less than eight hours later, shortly after ten a.m., wearing a filthy-looking John Deere ball cap. 'It's my lucky director's hat. It can never be washed.'

Ugh.

My dad was heading out for one of his epic runs and Mom was off to a yoga class. 'I always knew our cats had star quality,' she said when she heard the idea. 'I'm happy to help when I get back.'

I handed Dad his reflective vest and Mom her rape whistle. 'Don't forget to use my Christmas gifts.' They gave each other a look. 'I saw that. Better safe than sorry.'

After they left, Jacob showed me his digital camera.

It was small and lightweight, a gift from his parents. 'I guess we should talk about sets,' he said.

'Actually, I started working on something last night.' My mind had been abuzz with ideas for a cat-sized version of Catherine's bedroom at Wuthering Heights. Finally I'd given up on sleep altogether and padded down to our storage locker, careful to put my own rape whistle around my neck first. I'd rummaged around until I found three big boxes of my old crafting supplies, untouched since our move.

It took three separate trips to lug it all back upstairs. Everything was in those boxes, from paint to pipe cleaners. I even found the old bonnets Rachel and I had made during our *Little House on the Prairie* phase, and because no one could see me, I'd worn mine while I worked.

I took Jacob to my room and showed him what I'd created so far. It was a three-walled set made from a large cardboard box I'd found next to the recycling bins and decontaminated with Lysol, which gave it a faint lemony scent. I'd cut out a big window and hung fabric for curtains. I'd made miniature books and placed them on the windowsill as stand-ins for the books Lockwood needed to discover. Then I'd painted the walls ochre, to add to the moody, desolate feel of *Wuthering Heights*. I'd also dashed off a few drawings of cats in period costume and hung them around the room as portraits. 'I still need to make the bed,' I said. 'But it's big enough that we could probably fit one of the cat beds in.'

Jacob whistled. 'Wow, Petula. Did you get any sleep at all?'

'A bit. Not much.'

'You're really good.'

I let myself smile.

'Do you think we could get the cats to wear costumes?' Jacob asked.

'We can try. One of those boxes has a pile of dolls' clothes I made when I was younger.'

Jacob started rooting through the box, pulling out things he thought might be useful, while I put the finishing touches on the set. 'Hey. Is this Rachel?'

He held up a handmade mosaic frame with a photo of Rachel and me from a couple of years ago. We'd just taken a batik course, and we were wearing matching batik dresses and grinning from ear to ear. Maxine and Owen sat on our laps in batik T-shirts. Rachel still had thick, long dirty-blonde hair.

I took the photo from Jacob and placed it back in the box, facedown.

'What happened between you two?'

I didn't answer.

'Did she pull away after Maxine died?'

I shook my head.

'So?'

'So, none of your business.'

'OK. You're protecting your friend. I respect that.'

I looked away, too gutless to tell him I was protecting myself.

When my parents got home, Jacob enlisted their help. He made Mom our casting director–slash–cat wrangler. She cast Ferdinand as Lockwood and Anne of Green Gables as Catherine, 'because they're by far the most placid and malleable.' Alice was given the role of Heathcliff, and Stanley, the maid. My dad agreed to voice both Heathcliff and Lockwood, which he did with cheesy English accents. I voiced the women.

We had to shoot two scenes. The first was manageable: Lockwood gets led to the never-used room by the maid. We had to get the two cats to walk side by side down a hall, Stanley wearing a maid's cap and Ferdinand a bow tie. It took an hour, but eventually Jacob got what he needed.

The second scene had a lot of parts. Lockwood lies in bed reading Catherine's diaries and drifts off to sleep. A branch bangs on the window and when he tries to adjust it, Catherine's ghost-hand grabs his wrist. Lockwood's screams bring Heathcliff running. When he hears of the apparition he goes to the window and begs ghost-Catherine to return.

It took us the rest of the day to film. We were literally herding cats. Ferdinand kept clawing his nightshirt off and Anne of Green Gables took a stealth poop on the prop bed. All the cats wandered out of frame. We spent two hours on the final shots alone, because Alice did not want to wear her nightcap *or* look out the window. Eventually we fired her and replaced her with Moominmamma.

When we were finally done filming it was past six o'clock. Jacob started packing up to go home.

'Hang on,' said my dad. He walked over to the crammed floor-to-ceiling shelves and started searching through his records. He handed Jacob an album. 'In case you need some music. It's actually called "Wuthering Heights". It was released as a single in 1978. A song from Catherine's perspective. Kate Bush was only eighteen when she wrote it.'

Then my dad did something he hadn't done in two years.

He put the album on the record player and dropped the needle.

We all listened to the haunting song.

That night at supper the three of us went over every second of the day. Dad didn't jump up from the table immediately after he'd finished eating. We didn't lapse into awkward silences.

I was feeling something I hadn't felt in a long time. So long, in fact, that it took me a while to figure out what it was.

Happiness.

THIRTEEN

It was Antarctica cold in the counselling suite on Friday. I wore my cat hat and my Belgian flag scarf. Jacob kept his ridiculous orange parka on. We were the only two who seemed affected by the subzero temperatures, however. Alonzo wore a diaphanous white blouse and tight black leather trousers. Ivan sat beside him in a shiny red tracksuit, his black hair matted and bed-headed even though it was two p.m. Koula wore a tight tank top with MY EYES ARE UP HERE emblazoned in gold across her boobs and an arrow pointing up. This was paired with dangerously low-rise jeans. Every time she bent over (which was a full three times before she finally settled into her seat) she showed off an upper-ass tattoo that read BEATIFUL TRADGEDY.

It was a tragedy, all right.

'I call this one the Healing Heart,' Betty said. Her suit was a vibrant orange. 'I've created this huge construction-paper heart, which I'm going to cut into five pieces. You can get as creative as you like with yours, but the idea is to convey a regret. You can paint your heart, create a collage, write a poem, whatever you like. Then we'll piece the heart back together with these.' She held up a box of Dora the Explorer Band-Aids.

Ivan started kicking the underside of the table.

'How often do we need to say it?' said Koula. 'We're. Not. Six.'

Betty just gave her the death stare. 'Remember what we've talked about. More openness, less cynicism. Don't make me bring out the Jar.' Whenever one of us swore or said something nasty, Betty made us put a quarter into a large mason jar.

Seriously.

She picked up a pair of scissors and cut up the heart, handing us each a large piece. We all got down to work. Even Koula settled into it, but only after Betty took away her phone.

My drawing didn't take long. It was a button, simple and to the point. Ivan finished his next. Betty had gone into her office, so he grabbed the scissors and started jabbing them into the tabletop for entertainment, leaving little pockmarks in the wood.

Jacob noticed. 'Hey, Ivan, want to see what my hand can do?'

Ivan nodded. Jacob tickled Ivan under the chin and ruffled his hair – he even pretended to put a bionic finger up Ivan's nose. The scissors were forgotten; Ivan was enthralled. 'You're like Jaime Lannister from *Game of Thrones*.'

'Except my hand is way cooler than his. And I'm better-looking.'

Koula, who was hunched over her drawing, snorted.

'Want to hear a joke?' Jacob asked.

Ivan nodded.

'What do you call a man with no arms and no legs in a hole?'

I groaned. 'Seriously? That's so old.'

'Doug,' said Jacob.

It took Ivan a moment. Then he started to laugh.

I had never heard him laugh.

'What do you call a man with no arms and no legs on a wall?' Jacob continued. 'Art. What do you call a man with no arms and no legs in a pool? Bob.'

Ivan was laughing so hard, he had to hold his stomach.

'Old *and* offensive,' I said.

'I'm an amputee,' Jacob replied. 'I'm allowed.'

Betty returned to the table. 'All right, who would like to share first?'

'I'll go,' said Koula. Her drawing was in charcoal. She was depicted at the centre, with a bunch of angry faces circling her. 'I pissed off so many people when I was drunk or high. Now none of them will talk to me.'

Because you have the personality of a jackal, I thought.

'Can you tell us how that makes you feel?' asked Betty.

'How do you think it makes me feel? Like crap! Stupidest question ever.'

Betty stood up and went back to her office. She returned a moment later, carrying the Jar. 'Pay up.'

'Screw you,' said Koula.

'Oops. Two quarters.'

'Bite me!'

'Three.'

'Bitch!'

'A dollar even.'

Koula glared at Betty. She extricated a dollar from her pocket and tossed it across the table.

'OK,' Betty said. 'Next.'

Alonzo showed us his piece. He'd cut out a black-and-white photo of a man carrying a rainbow flag. Over the image he had pasted letters that formed words. EVIL. ABBERATION. FAGGOT.

'Those are some of the kinder words my dad used when I came out,' he said. 'I'm trying hard to be proud of who I am. But sometimes . . .' He stopped. 'Sometimes this inner voice still says my dad is right. That I *am* an affront to God.'

Jacob patted Alonzo's shoulder and Koula wrapped her arms around him. 'I want to punch your dad in the nose,' she said.

'Me too,' I said, feeling a small connection to Koula for the first time.

'Please,' she snorted. 'You'd never have the guts. You'd be worried about a stranger's blood. You'd have to put on rubber gloves and a hazmat suit and a mask before you even tried.'

'We all know violence is never the answer,' Betty said. 'Alonzo, you're a good person. I hope that one day your dad will be able to get past his prejudices and open his heart.'

'And maybe one day pigs will fly,' he said.

'Why don't you tell us about someone or something who's a positive in your life right now?'

'Well, my aunt is great. And I have supportive friends.' Alonzo looked at Koula. 'And I've started taking this . . . well, it's sort of a movement class.'

'Like dance?' asked Koula.

'Sort of. It's something I've always wanted to do, so. Carpe diem, right?'

It was Jacob's turn next. Drawing wasn't his strong point. His picture was of two stick people on a cloud, and another stick person – him – down below, with a frowny face.

He told the others almost word for word what he'd told me, about the accident that had killed his friends.

'That sucks,' said Koula. 'Tell me the driver went to jail.'

'Yeah. For six months.'

'What a joke.'

It was almost dismissal time when Ivan slid his drawing across the table. In the background he'd drawn a bunch of people standing in front of a coffin. In the foreground he'd drawn a house. A boy was in the window.

The bell rang. 'Why don't we all stay a few extra minutes, hear from Ivan, and put the heart back together?' said Betty.

But Ivan just belched loudly and made a beeline for the door. The rest of us weren't far behind.

FOURTEEN

Ivan was already at the curb when the rest of us stepped outside. We watched as he hopped into a red Mazda with its engine idling under a sign that read TRAFFIC-CALMED AREA. PLEASE DON'T IDLE YOUR ENGINES. The man in the driver's seat – presumably Ivan's dad because he had the same mop of black hair – didn't turn his head when Ivan got in.

It was raining hard. We huddled under the roof's overhang. 'What was Ivan's drawing about?' asked Jacob.

'His mom drowned two summers ago,' said Alonzo. 'It's not really clear whether it was an accident, or . . .'

'Suicide,' Koula said. 'You of all people should be able to say that word, Alonzo. You're the expert.'

'Nope. Amateur. My attempt failed.'

'If you become an expert, I'll kill you.' Koula and Alonzo burst out laughing.

Jacob looked at me, startled; I just shook my head and shrugged.

'Ivan was eleven when it happened,' Alonzo continued. 'His grandparents thought he was too young to go to the funeral. So he stayed home with some old aunt.'

'He didn't get to go to his own mother's funeral?'

'Nope.'

'Harsh.'

'Kind of explains why he gets that look on his face sometimes,' said Koula. 'Like he could murder you in your sleep.'

We all nodded in agreement.

Alonzo looked at Koula. 'Want to make a run for the bus stop?'

'Sure.'

'Or we could go for coffee,' said Jacob.

Awkward silence. 'Um,' I said.

'Um, what?'

'We don't really do that.'

'Do what?'

'Hang out.'

'Why not?'

'We don't . . .'

'Like each other,' said Koula.

'I'm buying,' Jacob said.

Koula and Alonzo shared a look. 'Does that include fancy stuff? Like s'mores Frappuccinos?' asked Koula.

'Sure.'

'We're in.'

Jacob turned to me. 'Petula?'

I didn't answer right away. I was thinking about bathrooms. I had become very good at structuring my days around seldom having to use public toilets, which were like ground zero for germs, perverts, and unattended backpacks. I'd learned to pee right before leaving for school, and as long as I didn't drink a lot of water I could hold it till I got home.

Right now I needed to pee.

'Make up your mind, Grandma,' said Koula. 'It's freezing.'

Lovely. Now Jacob knew her nickname for me.

'We won't stay long,' said Jacob.

So I went, hoping Grandma's bladder could hold out a while longer.

JJ Bean was packed. The rain had sent everyone inside. It smelled damp and funky, and it was hot and noisy.

I froze just inside the doorway. Jacob noticed, because he took my mittened hands and placed them on his waist, then pushed his tall frame through the crowd to a free table by the window. I just held on and followed. 'Thanks,' I murmured. I tried to stay focused. I tried not to get distracted by the man at the next table who kept coughing without covering his mouth. Or the woman who kept coughing into her hand. *Elbow! You cough into your elbow!*

We talked about this and that. Or rather, they talked. I was finding it hard to concentrate. Even though I'd passed on coffee, my need to pee was reaching crisis point. I couldn't hold it much longer. I edged my way out of my chair, slipping my mittens back on so I wouldn't have to touch any surfaces with my bare flesh. 'I'll be right back.'

Koula smirked. 'No you won't.' She turned to Jacob. 'You watch. I guarantee she'll be in there for, like, ten minutes, making sure no one's lurking in the stalls, putting down one of those paper toilet seat covers even though I'd bet good money she's a hoverer, flushing the toilet with her elbow, using paper towels to open and close the doors. Et cetera.'

I had the urge to throw myself at her and start scratching her face. But it would be like David going after Goliath. Minus David's victory.

I went to the bathroom.

And for the record, I was only eight minutes.

I timed it.

Even though I hadn't had any coffee, I was feeling jangly when we got ready to leave. This was the first time I'd gone out with people my own age since Maxine died. Even if they weren't friends, even if one of them was possibly a psychopath, it hadn't been entirely awful.

I was just buttoning up my sou'wester when Koula said, 'Uh-oh, Grandma. Your twelve o'clock.'

I followed her gaze.

Rachel, the Girl Formerly Known as My Best Friend, was at the counter with Aleisha and Mahshid.

'Couldn't you get arrested right now?' Koula grinned. 'Like, doesn't she have a restraining order against you or something?'

I started sweating profusely, and not just because I had my sou'wester on. 'Shut up, Koula.'

'Ooh, good comeback.' She turned to Jacob. 'Rumour has it Grandma here went at her ex-bestie with a carving knife—'

'That's a total lie!' I shouted. People turned to stare. Including Rachel.

Our eyes locked. I saw the sadness in her gaze.

And the pity.

I pushed my way between the tables and the people and made it out onto the pavement, where I gulped the fresh air. I started fast-walking towards home. *Screw Koula. Screw Koula and her ugly misspelled tattoo!* My blood sounded like an ocean in my ears. I'd stopped focusing on my surroundings; I was just barrelling towards home. So I was completely unprepared when a hand gripped my shoulder. I swivelled and brought my knee up, hard.

'Aaaagh!'

I'd just kneed Jacob in the nuts.

He doubled over in pain. 'What'd you do that for?'

'Never, ever sneak up on a woman like that!'

'I didn't sneak! I was calling your name. Holy jeez . . . Lucky I pack to the left and you aim to the right.'

'Sorry.'

He attempted to stand, wincing as he did so. 'You want to tell me what really happened with Rachel?'

'I didn't go after her with a carving knife.'

'I figured as much.'

I took a deep breath and came out with it. 'I cut off her hair.'

'You *what*?'

'I was at her place, a few months after Maxine died.

We were making greeting cards. She had really long hair then. It was pulled back in a braid.' We started walking again. 'Owen was there. Her little brother. He and Max were the same age.' Tears started rolling, unbidden, down my face. 'Owen kept making Rachel laugh. Then he toddled over and gave Rachel a hug and curled up in her lap. I felt like they were rubbing it in my face. And I snapped. I picked up my scissors and I grabbed her braid and I cut it off.'

Jacob just shook his head, speechless for once.

'Owen started to scream. Their parents came running. Rachel just kept feeling the back of her head and looking at me with this mystified expression on her face. And the worst part is, I didn't even feel bad. I just thought, *Now you know what it feels like to lose something.*'

'And she never spoke to you again?'

'No, she did. She came over to our apartment a few nights later and said she forgave me. She still wanted to be friends. And I said to her . . .' I paused. 'I said awful things.' I wiped one mittened hand across my face. '*Then* she never spoke to me again.' We had arrived outside the Arcadia. 'Now you know the truth about me.'

'What truth?'

'That I'm not a good person.'

He was quiet for a moment. 'You really think that?'

'Sometimes, when I got mad at Maxine, I told her I wished I was still an only child.' There. Now he knew everything.

I heard a whirring sound. Jacob took my chin in his carbon fibre hand. He tilted my face upward. With his real hand, he wiped a bead of snot from my nose. I was totally disgusted, and a tiny bit moved. 'You're wrong, Petula. You're a good person. You're a much better person than I am.'

'I find that hard to believe.'

He looked like he was about to say something more. But instead he put his arms around me and held me close.

My body stiffened. My first instinct was to push him away.

But with my face pressed into the damp warmth of his orange parka, and the weight of his arms around me, my limbs started to relax. He held me like that for a long time. 'You are your own worst enemy, Petula Harriet De Wilde.'

I couldn't argue with him there.

FIFTEEN

'I need to know that you're actively trying to get them adopted, Virginia,' Dad said. I could hear him from my bedroom. I'd just looked up Rachel's number on my phone. I'd done this before, but I never pressed Call.

'I am. I'm building profiles today for the Vancouver Feline Rescue website.'

'Do I have your word?'

'Andreas, for God's sake—'

'We can barely afford the others, Virginia. You know this. The food, the litter, the vet bills – it adds up.'

I closed my door to block them out.

I took a great big inhale and pressed Call.

'Hey, this is Rachel, sorry I missed your call. Leave me a—'

I hung up. Had she really missed my call? Or had she seen my name on caller ID and made an executive decision?

When I came out of my room, Dad had left for his epic Sunday run and Mom was getting ready to go to yoga.

I heard a *ping*. It was such a rare sound that both Mom and I glanced around, puzzled. 'Oh,' I said. 'It's my phone.'

It was a text. *Rachel,* I thought.

But it wasn't Rachel. It was Jacob.

Finished editing video. Want to come for brunch and a viewing?

'Ooh, from the cute boy!' Mom had come up behind me and read my private text over my shoulder.

'Mother!'

'You're saying yes, right?'

'I don't know.'

'I think he likes you,' Mom said in a singsong voice.

'Please. As if.' With everything he knew about me, that was a scientific impossibility.

She picked up her purse. 'I wish you wouldn't under-estimate yourself, Tula. You're a beautiful young woman.'

'Mom, *stop*. He just wants to show me our assignment.'

'Fine. Then text him back and say yes.'

'I will,' I said. 'When you're gone.'

'Nope. Now.'

It was a standoff. Then my mother did a shocking thing.

She grabbed my phone from my hands and typed, *Love to. Address?*

'Don't you dare press Send. If you press Send, I will never speak to you again.'

She pressed Send.

'I'm doing this for your own good, sweetheart. You've shut yourself off from the world for far too long.'

A moment later, Jacob texted me his address. *See you in half an hour.*

Mom slipped on her boots and left, humming to herself.

Jacob's building was a modern low-rise condo, right on English Bay. It was just a handful of blocks from the Arcadia, but it felt like a world apart.

I stood across the street, trying to summon the courage to go in. The sun was out and the seawall was full of outdoor enthusiasts in a rainbow assortment of spandex. I couldn't believe how many rollerbladers and cyclists without helmets I saw. *If you have an accident your head will split open like a cantaloupe!* I wanted to shout.

Since I didn't want to jaywalk, I headed a block out of my way to the light and crossed. When I arrived outside the front doors I took a few deep, calming breaths.

The lobby was huge and airy, with an enormous modern chandelier hanging from the ceiling. Even though I could tell the place had been built with earthquake proofing, there was no way I'd be caught standing under that massive light fixture. I edged around it to a desk manned by a guy in a blazer. His name tag said SERGE. 'Serge the Concierge,' I said as he buzzed the Cohens' apartment. 'It's like it was destiny.'

He didn't crack a smile. 'They're expecting you,' he said. 'Sixth floor.'

I took the stairs. When I emerged, Jacob was waiting for me by the elevators. 'I don't do elevators,' I said, out of breath.

'Ah. I should have guessed. I don't, either.'

'Right. Confined spaces.'

I heard his bionic hand whir, and next thing I knew he'd plucked my cat hat from my head and put it on. 'I keep meaning to tell you, I love this hat.'

I tried to grab it back, but he dodged out of the way. 'Haven't you heard of lice?'

'You're accusing me of having lice?'

'Anyone can get lice.'

'Maybe you just gave *me* lice.'

'Impossible. I check my hair every week.'

'Of course you do.' He handed me back the hat. 'Did you make it?'

'Yes.'

'You're very talented, Petula.'

I felt my armpits get moist; I was having a teenage hot flash.

Jacob took me by the elbow and guided me down the hall. 'I'd love a hat like that. Would you make me one? Preferably a dog? I had a beagle back in Toronto.'

'Sorry. This is all old stuff. I don't knit any more.'

'Why not?'

Because the last thing I knitted was the wolf suit that killed my sister. 'I just don't.'

'Well, sure. If it's too complicated—'

'It's not too complicated. I'm a knitting champion. Won two contests. Over a thousand bucks in free wool.'

'Wow. So a dog hat should be a piece of cake.'

I was pretty sure I was being played.

He pushed open the door at the end of the hallway and we stepped inside.

The apartment was the exact opposite of mine, not in size but in newness. It had polished hardwood floors, high ceilings, and a wraparound balcony that overlooked the ocean. Best of all, it was neat as a pin.

Jacob's parents appeared from the kitchen. Mrs Cohen wore tights, a loose-fitting cashmere top, and big purple glasses. Mr Cohen was in jeans and a T-shirt, with a frilly apron that read WORLD'S OKAYEST COOK.

'Petula, nice to meet you,' said his mom. 'I'm Miranda, and this is David.' When we shook hands, I hoped they wouldn't notice that I'd left my mittens on.

We moved into their living/dining area. David served eggs Benedict. 'I'm not much of a cook, but I do a mean brunch,' he said. As we talked, I wolfed down my food, with the exception of one underdone egg, which I discreetly pushed to the side of my plate. No need to court salmonella poisoning.

David said, 'I hear you and my son shot a movie starring cats.'

'Yes.'

'It's so nice to see Jacob making movies again,' said Miranda. 'He used to do it all the time with—' She stopped.

I looked up. Jacob's jaw was clenched. Miranda looked close to tears. David looked anxiously from his wife to his son.

Jacob tossed his napkin on the table. 'Come on, Petula. I'll show you the video.'

'Thank you so much for brunch.' I started to clear my dishes, but David stopped me.

'It's OK. Leave them. We've got it covered.'

Jacob led me down the hallway. 'What just happened?' I asked.

'Nothing. I just don't like talking about the past, and they know it.'

We entered his room. It was like the rest of the apartment, neat and tidy. A massive DVD collection was stored on three bookshelves. Two framed movie posters hung on one wall, one for *Inglourious Basterds,* the other for *The Grand Budapest Hotel.* His digital camera sat on a shelf beside a handful of books on cinema and directing.

That was it. There were no photos, no trophies, no souvenirs, no knick-knacks.

Jacob pulled an extra chair up to his desk and we both sat down. His laptop was hooked up to a huge monitor, one of two.

We were so close, our knees grazed.

Then I felt his hand touch mine.

Sometimes the body has a response that the mind has zero control over. My mind didn't *want* my body to feel like jelly all of a sudden. I didn't *want* to have this overwhelming desire to lean into him, to feel his arms around me again.

Still. He was touching my hand. Was he sending a signal?

No.

It was his robot limb. A hunk of carbon fibre.

He had no idea his hand was touching mine.

SIXTEEN

Mr Herbert flipped on the lights. 'When I told you I wanted you to adapt a portion of the novel, I didn't mean I wanted you to make a mockery of it.'

It was Monday afternoon. Jacob and I stood at the front of the class. I'd decided to embrace my weirdo status and wore cat-themed clothing for the occasion, including my wire cat earrings, my cat hat and a kitten T-shirt, which I'd found in the dollar bin at the Goodwill and bedazzled with rhinestones. Jacob was more understated in his off-white fisherman's sweater and jeans.

Ours was the last presentation. We'd already sat through a few poorly acted scenes, a dull 'inner monologue', and a long, boring poem. Our *Cataptation* woke everyone from their stupor. The class – minus Mr Herbert – had laughed in all the right places.

Jacob had done an amazing job. His shots, combined with his editing skills, somehow made the whole thing work. He'd managed to make Moominmamma as Heathcliff look genuinely tormented when calling for Catherine at the window (she'd actually just been yawning), and Ferdinand as Lockwood appeared truly startled when the ghost of Catherine grabbed his paw. Even the lighting worked, and my sets looked better on-screen than they had in real life. Jacob had added sound effects and music and end credits. I felt a flutter of pleasure when I saw *Written by Petula H. De Wilde,* followed by *Directed by Jacob S. Cohen.*

'We didn't make a mockery,' Jacob said. 'We did what you asked for. We were creative.'

'I'm not sure that it falls into the realm of creativity. All right, next class Carla and Shen will present first—'

'I'm sorry,' Jacob interrupted. He was smiling, but I could see the muscles around his mouth tightening. 'I take exception to that. What Petula and I did was very creative. We thought outside the box.'

'And made a trite piece of fluff.'

'It wasn't trite. Funny, yes. Trite, no. Comedies always get short shrift. Happens at the Oscars all the time. Because it's funny, people mistake it for being easy.'

'That's enough, Mr Cohen. You and Ms De Wilde will take your seats.'

Jacob's face darkened. He clenched his hand.

'But, sir,' I said, 'everyone else loved it.'

Our classmates started clapping and hooting, including Alonzo and, I noted with a stab of delight, Rachel.

'See?' I said. 'The people have spoken.'

'*The people* as a collective aren't known for their good taste,' said Mr Herbert. 'Hence billions still served at McDonald's. Hence high ratings for shows like *Keeping Up With the Kardashians* and *Real Housewives*.'

'Wow,' said Jacob. 'I think you just insulted the entire class.' There were angry murmurs of agreement.

'Enough!' said Mr Herbert. 'Sit down, both of you.'

Jacob strode back to his seat, taut with anger. I let my impulsiveness get the better of me, because suddenly I shouted, 'Those who can, do! Those who can't, teach!'

The class erupted with laughter.

And I was sent to the office.

'That was not a nice thing to say,' Mr Watley said to me ten minutes later. He was trying hard to look stern, but his whole body shook with barely suppressed laughter. I'd just shown him the video, which I had on a USB stick.

'You're right, sir.' I sat across from him in my favourite chair. 'It wasn't. And to be fair, most teachers *can*. I'm just not sure Mr Herbert is one of them.'

'We've talked about your impulsive behaviour, Petula. Apologise to him for your outburst. And try to control yourself from now on.' Mr Watley stood, signalling the end of our meeting.

'That's it?'

He shrugged. 'The two of you made an excellent film. Unfortunately, I'm not the one who will grade you.'

I stood up.

'Oh, and one more thing. I'm glad your partnership with Mr Cohen worked out so well.' He looked at me with a very smug grin.

'Is that your way of saying "I told you so", sir?'

He patted his comb-over. 'Yes, Petula. Yes, it is.'

Classes had already been let out by the time I left Mr Watley's office. I grabbed my coat from my locker and headed outside. It was a decent early-February day; I'd even seen a snowdrop poking its head out of the earth on my way to school. It was almost enough to fill a pessimist like me with a sense of renewal and hope.

I spotted Jacob standing on the pavement, his orange parka over his arm. He was surrounded by a group of people from our English class. Popular people. Including Rachel.

You could join them. Just walk over there right now. Go. Go now.

But my legs wouldn't move.

I was no longer one of them. And maybe a sick part of me had hoped Jacob wasn't one of them, either.

But he wasn't like me. He was still an outgoing, gregarious person.

I knew how it would play out. He'd still be nice to me. He'd say hi in the halls. But after a while he'd have a hard time remembering my name. Eventually he'd start calling me Petunia again.

The beginning of the end of our friendship was unfolding before my eyes.

Jacob waved me over.

I pretended I didn't see him and headed towards home. It was easier this way, for both of us.

I hummed 'All by Myself', by Eric Carmen, as I walked. Dad and I had listened to that schmaltzy song dozens of times. When I was a couple of blocks from the Arcadia I heard footsteps coming up fast behind me. I tightened my fingers around my keys and whipped around, fist poised, knee at the ready.

'Don't even think of kneeing me in the balls again,' Jacob said, out of breath. We reached a stoplight. 'I was waiting for you outside. Didn't you see me waving?' He glanced both ways, then started crossing the street on a red light.

I grabbed his arm. 'Please don't do that!'

'Petula, there's nothing coming. Not a car in sight.' But he waited with me until the light turned green. 'You were amazing in class. I'm just sorry you got sent to the office. What happened?'

'Nothing, really. Mr Watley thought the short was awesome too.'

Jacob laughed. 'It *is* awesome! You should've heard some of the compliments we got. Including from Rachel.'

'You can stop now,' I said.

'Stop what?'

'This. The assignment's done. You don't have to hang out with me any more.'

He stared at me for a long time. 'Wow. I knew your self-esteem was in the toilet. But this is a new low, even for you.'

'This isn't about self-esteem. It's just life.'

'You ever see the Debbie Downer sketches on *Saturday Night Live*?'

'You're comparing me to Debbie Downer?'

'You have some great qualities, Petula. But this maudlin, self-pitying, "the world's going to hell in a handbasket" thing you've got going on is definitely not one of them.'

Ouch!

'And while we're at it, can I just say that Rachel seems like a great person? A forgiving person. So why not just man up and talk to her?'

'Because I'm not a man?'

'Then *woman* up. Say you're sorry. You actually have the chance to make amends here, because *she's still alive*. Which is more than I can say for my friends.' And on that note, he turned and walked away with his giraffelike stride.

'I am not maudlin and self-pitying!' I shouted after him.

Feeling very sorry for myself.

I stomped into the apartment and tore off my coat. Mom was already home; her red boots were next to the bench. A bunch of the cats surrounded me, meowing in greeting.

'Have the cats been fed?' I called.

There was no answer.

'Mom?'

Still no answer. I headed down the hall to her bedroom.

The blinds were drawn. Ferdinand and Stuart Little were curled up like sentries at the top of the bed. I could just make out a lump under the quilt, and tufts of wavy chestnut hair. Even though I'd been through this a handful of times before, anxiety still rose in my throat like a hard rubber ball. 'Mom?'

'Hi, Tula,' came her muffled response.

I let myself exhale. I hadn't really believed she was dead, but still, it was a relief. 'You OK?'

'Think I came down with something at work.'

I felt her forehead. It wasn't hot.

I fed the cats. I vacuumed. I threw in a load of laundry. I uncovered another of Anne of Green Gables' stealth turds and cleaned it up. I made dinner. I tried to get Mom to eat, but she wasn't hungry.

Dad wouldn't be back for hours, which was good. It upset him when she got like this. By the time he came home it would just look like she'd gone to bed early.

I lay down next to Mom and spooned her. She held my hands against her heart.

'She was such a lovely little girl.'

'She was. I'm so sorry, Mom.'

'You have nothing to be sorry for. No one blames you. You know this.'

Except I don't.

When I knew Mom was asleep, I got up and went to my room. Jacob's comments started tumbling through my head again. I tried to feel angry. But a part of me knew he wasn't entirely wrong.

I tried to read, but I couldn't concentrate, so I searched online for articles for my scrapbook.

Boy Gets Pogo Stick for Birthday, Dies on First Jump

A ten-year-old boy in Auckland, New Zealand, has died after receiving his dream gift from his parents. 'He'd begged them for a pogo stick,' a saddened neighbour said. The boy tried to jump on the pogo stick and fell off, hitting his head on a rock . . .

Man Killed by Falling Air Conditioner

Forty-three-year-old Kent Tremay was on his way to his girlfriend's house to propose to her, say friends, when a loose air-conditioning unit became dislodged from an apartment window and fell eight storeys, hitting Tremay . . .

But I didn't print them because I knew Jacob would say my scrapbook fell into the Debbie Downer category.

'You don't know me,' I muttered. I always had much better comebacks when my conversations were one way. 'You have no idea what I'm capable of.' To prove it, I picked up my phone and wrote Rachel a text.

Can we talk?

This time, I pressed Send.

SEVENTEEN

I arrived outside school at exactly 7:55 the next morning. The bagel I'd forced myself to eat kept rising in my throat.

Rachel had texted me back just as I'd been drifting off to sleep: *Picnic benches. 8:00 tomorrow morning.*

She was already there, bundled up in a thick wool coat and grey-and-white snowflake scarf. I had the same scarf in red and white; we'd knit them together. 'Hello,' I said, my voice cracking.

'Hi.' It was weird to see her up close again. I noticed that her blonde hair had grown to her shoulders; it was held back with a handmade purple-and-white polka-dot headband, which matched her handmade purple-and-white polka-dot tote bag.

I was wearing a couple of items that Rachel had made for me: a multicoloured belt crafted from old ties, and the meant-for-special-occasions-only bottle-cap necklace.

I sat down beside her. It was cool and damp, but it wasn't raining.

Rachel didn't say a word. It was my job to get things started. 'I like your headband. It's very *Jane Fonda Workout*.'

'Thanks.'

'Did you get the idea—'

'From Wendy Russell on *The Marilyn Denis Show*? Yes.'

'I saw that episode, too. It was a good one.'

Rachel nodded, and we grew silent.

'Might I also say that your dickey is spectacular?'

She glanced down at her mock turtleneck in kelly green. 'Thanks. I made it last week out of a piece of old fleece.' More silence. I undid a couple of toggles on my coat and angled myself so Rachel could see the necklace. 'Oh,' she said. 'That's supposed to be for special occasions.'

'I guess I thought, you know, this had the potential to be one.'

She looked away.

'How are you?' I asked.

'Good.'

'And your parents?' I omitted the remaining member of her family.

'They're good, too. How about yours?'

'I honestly don't know how to answer that.' And suddenly, inexplicably, I felt tears spring to my eyes. Rachel reached out and put a hand over mine, and I saw she was wearing the Miss Piggy mittens I'd made her for Christmas three years earlier. 'I'm so sorry, Rachel. You were trying so hard to be a good friend, and I was such an awful one.'

'Truly awful.'

'What I did— What I said—'

'I could have lived with what you did. But the other . . .'

'I know. I don't know what to say. I was so angry, I was . . . spewing hatred.' I forced my next words out. 'How's your brother?'

Rachel smiled. 'He's great. Super excited to start kindergarten next year, talking a mile a minute, very opinionated . . .'

It felt like my heart was being squeezed.

'Just last week he rode his bike without training wheels . . .'

I couldn't help it. I started to cry for real.

Rachel stopped. 'I'm so sorry. Oh, Petula, I'm so sorry.' Then she was crying, too. 'I still miss her so much. She was such an awesome little girl.'

We let ourselves be sad for a while. 'I brought you something,' I said eventually. I rummaged around in my tote bag and pulled out our *Little House on the Prairie* bonnets.

Rachel started to laugh. 'Oh my God . . .'

We put them on. Then, spontaneously, we started acting out our all-time favourite scene, when poor Mary Ingalls discovers she's blind. 'Help me, Pa!' we said in unison. 'Pa, I can't see! Hold me! It's dark! It's too dark! I'm scared, Pa!'

Kids had started to arrive for school. They stared openly. Koula strode past in her Doc Martens and fishnet stockings. 'Freaks!' she yelled.

But I couldn't care less. It was a seriously awesome moment. Like we'd travelled back in time. 'I hate that Nellie Oleson!' I shouted, quoting another of our favourite lines. 'I hate that Nellie Oleson!' I said again, waiting for Rachel to join in.

But she didn't. Her expression had gotten all serious again. She pulled off the bonnet and held it out to me.

'You can keep it,' I said. 'It's yours.'

She hesitated before she stuffed it into her school bag. 'I guess I should go.' Her voice had taken on an edge that I did not like.

'Um. I was hoping—'

'Hoping we could pick up where we left off?'

'No. Maybe.'

'Why would you want to be friends with a fat, ugly loser who can't see that everyone around her hates her guts and thinks she's pathetic?'

'I didn't say that.'

'You did. But that wasn't the worst of it, Petula. You also said –' her voice caught – 'you said the wolf suit was my idea. You said Maxine's death was my fault.'

'Rachel,' I pleaded, 'I wasn't myself. I was a mess. I was medicated.'

'I know. I know all that. But it's not that easy to forget.' She looked at the ground. 'What I went through doesn't come close to what you went through, what you *are* going through. But you really hurt me, Petula. You made me feel like garbage.'

'You were never the garbage. *I'm* the garbage.'

The bell rang. Rachel stood. 'I'm glad you reached out. Really. Let's . . . let's just see how it goes.' Then she walked away.

I felt like my guts were lying on the pavement in front of me.

I sat there for a long time. I don't know what I'd expected. I was so shell-shocked I barely registered the red Mazda that squealed up to the curb, fifteen minutes after classes had started. I barely registered the boy in the shiny blue Adidas tracksuit until he sat down beside me and started punching my arm.

'Ow. Ivan, stop.'

'Sorry. I just wanted you to see me.'

I don't know why, but that made me feel even more gutted. 'I see you.'

'You look sad.'

'I feel sad.'

'Yeah. Me too.'

We sat in silence for a few more minutes. 'I guess we should get to class,' I said. We both stood up. Being a good six inches taller than him, I gazed right down at his terrible bed head. 'Hang on.' I grabbed a comb from my tote bag. 'Do you mind?'

Ivan shrugged. He turned around, and I combed out the back of his hair. It was super greasy. I felt the bagel rise in my throat again, but I got the job done. 'There. That's better.'

He broke into a huge grin. 'Thanks, Petula.'

'You're welcome, Ivan.'

When I entered the building I went straight to the girls' washroom. I threw my comb in the garbage and scrubbed my hands under scalding-hot water for two full rounds of 'Happy Birthday'.

EIGHTEEN

I didn't see Jacob until Friday at Crafting for Crazies; he'd been absent all week. I took a seat as far from him as possible, still stung by his Debbie Downer remark. At least Koula wasn't there, I noted with relief.

I was in a crappy mood. My encounter with Rachel still stung, big-time. Since our talk she'd made a point of smiling at me and saying 'hi' in the halls, but the casual friendliness was almost worse than no friendliness.

Betty joined us, wearing a banana-yellow suit. She looked like Big Bird's little sister. 'I have what I hope will be an especially fun assignment for you today.' She pulled a package of Costco tube socks from her bag and tossed it onto the table.

We stared at the package, confused.

'Sock puppets,' she said.

Alonzo laughed. Betty didn't. 'Wait,' he said. 'You're serious?'

Suddenly the door burst open and Koula walked in.

'If you'd let me explain,' Betty continued as Koula sat down with a thud. 'The idea is that you can decorate the socks and create a completely unique persona. Then you can use the puppets to express your true feelings. You'd be surprised how much more truthful you can be when you speak through a conduit.'

We were dead quiet.

Betty tore open the package and tossed us each a sock. 'Remember our motto: Less cynicism, more openness. At least give it a try.' She put a sock on her own hand. 'See?' she said in a high-pitched voice. 'It's not that hard.'

We all rolled a sock onto our hands. Jacob got some help from Ivan.

'Who would like to start?' said Betty's puppet.

Koula lifted her sock-clad hand. 'Koula tried to visit her mom last night.' Her puppet spoke in a seriously creepy Oscar the Grouch–meets–Freddy Krueger voice. 'Koula wanted to say sorry. When her mom saw who it was, she wouldn't open the door. So Koula started kicking it and yelling, "Bitch, let me in!" But she wouldn't!'

'And this surprises Koula?' I, or rather my sock puppet, asked.

Koula stood up. 'Shut your piehole, Grandma,' her sock puppet said.

My sock puppet got right in her sock puppet's face. 'You shut *your* piehole! Tell Koula to quit telling people I went after Rachel with a carving knife. Tell her I think she's a psycho bitch!'

Koula dropped her hand and put her face inches from mine. 'Don't call me a psycho bitch, bitch!'

I recoiled from the smell.

She reeked of booze.

Betty smelled it, too. 'Koula, you've been drinking.'

Koula lifted her sock puppet. 'Koula has not.'

'I'm not stupid.'

'Could've fooled Koula,' said her sock puppet.

'Don't make me get the Jar—'

'You think you're helping us with these lame-ass baby projects, but you're not.' Koula swivelled the puppet to look at the rest of us. 'Well? Is Koula right, or is she right?'

Betty cast her cool gaze on the rest of us.

We all raised our hands.

'She's right,' said our sock puppets.

'Told you!' Koula raised her socked fist triumphantly

and lost her balance. We watched in horror as she fell face-first on the carpeted floor.

'Mrrmph,' she moaned. Then she started to cry. Wail, actually. Mascara ran down her cheeks in two dark lines.

For the first time, unflappable Betty looked flapped.

Alonzo squatted down beside Koula and stroked her hair. 'Oh, Koula. Drunk *and* maudlin. What a winning combo.'

Koula let loose with a string of swearwords. Then, her wailing ceased as suddenly as it had begun.

She'd passed out.

'Help me get her up,' said Betty.

We tried to get Koula to standing position, but she was a dead weight. Instead, Alonzo and I positioned ourselves by her shoulders, while Jacob and Ivan positioned themselves at her feet. 'On the count of three. One, two, three.'

We hoisted Koula and carried her to Betty's office, where we laid her on the love seat. Betty put a blanket on top of her, then turned to the rest of us. 'You don't like my assignments, and that's fine. So here's my challenge to you. Come up with your own project. Present the idea to me next week.' Then she pushed us out of her office and closed the door.

NINETEEN

The funeral was Jacob's idea. 'Ivan, in your drawing, your regret was not being able to go to your mom's funeral. Well, maybe you can. Maybe we can create one for you.'

'How?' Ivan asked. We were sitting at JJ Bean, minus Koula, and Ivan was slurping a huge peppermint hot chocolate.

'Does she have a gravesite?'

'Yeah. At Mountain View Cemetery.'

'So, we'll go there.'

'And do what exactly?' Alonzo clutched a latte. He sounded skeptical.

'Go through the rituals. It'll be like performance art.

I can film it.' Jacob turned to Ivan. 'You'll have the video as a keepsake. It'll be something you can watch any time you want.'

Ivan was still trying to wrap his mind around the concept. 'Can I talk about her? Like, memories and stuff?'

'Absolutely. You can deliver the eulogy. Say a proper goodbye.'

Ivan's eyes lit up. He had a big whipped cream moustache. 'I like this idea.'

When Jacob pitched the idea to Betty the following Friday, she also liked it.

I was the only one who hated it.

The last time I'd been to a cemetery, we'd buried Maxine. I remember very little from that day. When I picture it, we are enveloped in fog, although apparently it was clear and sunny. I remember my dad and his sister, who'd flown in from Antwerp, having to hold my mom up because her knees kept buckling. I remember murmurs of relatives I barely knew. 'Such a tragedy . . .' 'Home alone with her sister . . .' 'Death of a child . . .' 'Never recover . . .'

I remember my sister's tiny coffin.

That image gets replayed a lot.

And I remember the sound my mom and dad made when the coffin was lowered into the ground.

So hanging out at a cemetery on a Saturday night – the date everyone had agreed to – was not my idea of a good time. I thought about bailing.

Then I thought about Ivan, and how much this meant to him.

Then I thought about bailing again.

Then I thought about Ivan.

And on it went.

I was still agonising over it when Jacob arrived at seven to pick me up. He wore a tailored grey suit with a black wool coat on top. 'Wow,' I blurted. 'You look nice. I mean, aside from that.' He also wore his filthy John Deere cap.

'I'm sure you look nice too, under all those layers. At the moment you look like the Michelin Man's twin.'

I wore a dark blue skirt, thick wool tights, and a white top. I'd pulled on two bulky sweaters, followed by my pea coat, cat hat, mittens, and Belgian flag scarf. The last thing I needed was to catch some new strain of flu virus.

I grabbed my dad's reflective vest from the hall closet.

'You're not actually putting that on.'

I wrestled it on over my other layers. 'It's pitch-dark out. This way I can be seen. You, on the other hand – a car would never see you. You'd be roadkill.' I picked up my backpack, which was heavy with supplies.

Jacob grabbed it. 'Allow me.'

I yelled goodbye to my parents and followed him out the door.

I did a deep-breathing exercise as we walked to the bus stop.

'You OK?' asked Jacob.

'Yes. Why?'

'You sound like Darth Vader.'

I wasn't about to tell him that on top of everything else, I hadn't set foot on a bus in two years. 'Oh, I almost forgot. I have something for you to try on.' I rummaged around in my backpack and pulled out a half-finished beagle hat.

'No way. You did it.'

'Yes.' My boxes of old crafting supplies were still in my bedroom, so a few nights earlier I'd forced myself to dig out some knitting needles and balls of wool. I felt anxious, but once I got started, it felt fine. Good, even. Like riding a bike, even if I would never again ride a bike. 'I need to see if it's the right size.'

He sat down on the bus shelter bench. I stood behind him and put the hat on his head. 'I think I'm going to need to make it bigger. Your cranium is massive.'

'It holds a very big brain.'

I held the hat in place. His hair was supersoft and shiny.

I wanted to run my hands through it. Instead I leaned in carefully and sniffed. His head smelled like Ivory soap and breakfast sausages.

Delicious.

I had an overwhelming urge to bury my lips in his hair. The voice inside my brain was goading me on. *Do it! He won't even notice.* I knew it was madness, but I leaned in closer. Closer. My lips were almost touching his hair—

'Here's our bus.' Jacob stood up, and I narrowly avoided losing my front teeth.

It took me for ever to pay the fare because I didn't dare remove my mittens and touch any of the bus's surfaces with my bare hands. Finally Jacob grabbed my wallet and took out the correct change.

We walked towards the back. I wrapped my scarf over my mouth. Jacob shook his head. 'Maybe we should roll you up in layers of bubble wrap. Poke a few holes in it so you can breathe.'

'Ha-ha.' It came out muffled.

We found two seats near the back. I do not understand why buses don't come equipped with seat belts. It's just common sense.

I started another deep-breathing exercise. Aside from

my loud inhalations and exhalations, we made the journey in silence.

Ivan was waiting for us when we got off the bus. He wore a shiny black tracksuit. 'It's the best I could do,' he said. 'My mom bought it for me.'

'That makes it perfect,' said Jacob.

Koula and Alonzo stepped off another bus a few minutes later. Koula was meant to be grounded, but her dad was attending a Greek Cultural Society banquet and wouldn't be home till late, so she'd snuck out. She wore a short black dress with black fishnet tights, red Doc Martens, and a black bomber jacket. Her nose still showed signs of rug burn from her fall. 'I brought flowers,' she said, her voice subdued. She held up a limp bouquet of carnations dyed a garish blue. 'You said blue was your mom's favourite colour.'

It was becoming harder to completely hate her.

As we headed towards the cemetery entrance I fell into step beside her. 'How are you doing?'

'Meh,' she said. 'But thanks for asking.'

We arrived at the entrance. We'd worked out all the final details of our plan at YART – Alonzo had even made a checklist – but we'd forgotten one thing.

Opening hours.

The gates to the cemetery were locked. A six-foot-high wrought iron fence ran along the perimeter.

'Crap!' Ivan's cheeks puffed out. He looked like he was about to burst into tears.

I put a hand on his shoulder, secretly relieved. 'It's OK. We can come back another time.'

'But I'm all ready! I have things to say!'

'Ivan, you can climb, right?' asked Jacob. Ivan nodded. My heart froze as I understood what Jacob was suggesting. 'I'll go first.'

Jacob started to climb the fence. It took him a while with his robotic hand, but by using his left hand to pull himself up, he eventually made it to the top. He jumped down to the other side. Alonzo helped Ivan over, then Koula.

Then it was my turn.

I was terrified.

Alonzo gave me a boost. I started to climb. With all my layers, it wasn't easy. I'm pretty sure I whimpered. When I got to the top I perched there, my feet dangling over the other side. The earth seemed a long way away.

Jacob held out his arms. 'I'll catch you.'

I didn't move.

'It's OK. You can trust me.'

I closed my eyes. I jumped.

And he did catch me, sort of. The sheer mass of my five-foot-eleven body landing on his made him stumble and fall backwards, but he never let go of me. I landed on top of him, my face centimetres from his.

I started to laugh. I'd leapt from a fence! I felt like Wonder Woman!

'Oh my God, you'd think you'd just climbed Mount Everest,' said Koula. 'Get over yourself, Grandma.'

'My mom was a great lady. She always put a treat in my lunch, like a Twinkie or a bag of chips. Or Cheez-Its. She knew I loved Cheez-Its.' Ivan was delivering his eulogy. We stood by a simple marble headstone that read IVANKA BOGDANOVICH, BELOVED DAUGHTER, MOTHER, AND WIFE. 'And she only yelled at me when I deserved it. And she only smacked me when I was really out of control.'

Alonzo and I shared a look, but Koula nodded like this made sense. Jacob stood a few feet away, filming.

Ivan started talking directly to the tombstone. 'We miss you, Mom. Dad's doing OK. He drinks a lot of beer. And vodka.' He started to cry. Because I was so layered up I figured I could safely put an arm around him. 'You knew you weren't a great swimmer, so I'll never know why you swam out so far, and that's hard.' He wiped his sleeve across his nose and I did my best not to shudder. 'I miss you every single day.'

Poor Ivan. He wasn't a demon. He was just a kid who'd lost the person who was most important to him in the world. I wrapped my other arm around him. If he got snot on me it would only be on Dad's reflective vest. I could put it through a hot-water wash.

Alonzo pulled out a speech he'd printed from the Internet and began to read. 'Because God has chosen to call our sister from this life to Himself, we commit her body to the earth, for we are dust and unto dust we shall return.'

I unzipped my backpack and pulled out a collapsible shovel. Ivan took it and dug a small, discreet hole next to Ivanka's tombstone. Then I lifted out the miniature coffin–slash–memory box I'd made for the occasion. I'd lined an old Converse shoe box with purple velour and written Ivanka's name in calligraphy on the lid.

'That's really nice, Petula,' said Ivan. He opened his own pack and started taking out items one by one. 'This is a Mother's Day card I made for her when I was five. This is a stone I gave her, because it looked like a heart. This is a photo of the two of us together in Mexico. Before she . . . Well.' He placed the items into the box.

He put the lid on and laid the box in the hole. Then he shovelled the dirt back in place and patted it down.

Jacob caught it all on camera. Including the blinding beam of light that suddenly engulfed us. 'What the hell do you kids think you're doing?'

A large security guard stood on the roadway, aiming his flashlight at us. 'Good evening, sir,' Jacob began. 'I can explain—'

The guard didn't let him finish. 'You're not supposed to be here. I'm calling the cops.' He pulled out his phone.

Jacob lowered his camera. 'Run.'

We split into two groups. Jacob, Ivan, and I went left; Koula and Alonzo went right.

The guard chose to run after Jacob, Ivan, and me. For a large guy, he was surprisingly fast. We tore through the cemetery, weaving among tombstones. In retrospect, my reflective vest was perhaps a bad choice; I made for a very visible target.

I was worried I was going to pee my tights, but Ivan was having the time of his life, laughing as we ran. Jacob was still holding his camera up.

'You're filming this?' I said.

'Of course! This is solid gold!'

We arrived at the fence, panting. Jacob shoved his camera into his pocket. He gave Ivan a boost over, then me. I hesitated when I reached the top; Jacob wasn't there to catch me on the other side. But I could see the guard bearing down on us. So I jumped.

I landed on my knees, hard.

Jacob started to climb the fence, but his bionic hand slowed him down. The security guard was closing in.

Jacob reached the top of the fence just as the guard arrived, wheezing and out of breath. He grabbed Jacob's foot. 'Gotcha!'

But all he got was Jacob's shoe. Jacob wriggled his foot free and dropped to the other side. 'We're sorry to have caused you any trouble,' he said. 'We weren't being disrespectful, you have my word. We were just helping someone grieve.'

The guard looked taken aback.

'I don't suppose you'd toss me my shoe?' Jacob asked.

The guard looked at the shoe in his hands, still catching his breath. Then he shrugged and threw it over the fence.

Jacob caught it. 'Thanks.'

We heard sirens in the distance. We had no idea whether or not they were for us, but we didn't wait to find out.

We started running again. Over his shoulder, Jacob hollered, 'Have a good night!'

Jacob and I got back to the Arcadia an hour later. He knelt to check on my torn tights and banged-up knees.

'Be sure to put disinfectant on when you get upstairs.'

I blame what happened next on the endorphins still coursing through my body.

As he straightened, I put my hands on his shoulders and kissed him.

On the lips.

He pulled back.

'Sorry. I'm so sorry. I don't know what made me—'

He took hold of my wrist. He pulled me close.

This time, he kissed me.

My experience with kissing up to now went like this:

1) An awful, spittle-filled attempt at tonguing by a boy during a game of spin the bottle.
2) Pecks on the cheek by male relatives.

But even so, I knew that this kiss felt right, and good. So good that when thoughts of saliva-transmitted illnesses like mononucleosis and oral herpes crept into my brain, I was able to push most of them out.

I replaced them with these thoughts instead:

Jacob is not 'this side of' good-looking.

He is spectacular.

TWENTY

I couldn't stop humming 'Walking on Sunshine', by Katrina and the Waves the next morning. Normally I pooh-poohed that song, because if you actually walked on sunshine you'd be burned to a crisp. But it would not leave my head.

'Someone's in a good mood,' Dad said as we finished breakfast. He was wearing his Billie Holiday T-shirt. Mom was in one of her favourites, too: I LIKE BIG BOOKS AND I CANNOT LIE.

'I take it you had fun last night?' she said. Ferdinand was stretched out on her lap.

I smiled and nodded. 'What did you two wind up doing?' I asked. It had been the first time in ages that they'd had the place to themselves.

'I read the new Kate Atkinson,' said Mom.

'I alphabetised my records,' said Dad.

'Seriously?'

Neither of them would look at me, or at each other. Dad stood up. 'Time for me to head into the office. I have—'

'A lot of paperwork, yeah, yeah, yeah. You two do remember your twentieth wedding anniversary is coming up fast, right?'

Their nineteenth had been a bust. Mom had given Dad a book on barbecuing, when we didn't have a balcony or a barbecue. She'd obviously picked it up last minute from work. Dad hadn't given Mom anything, not even a card.

'We remember,' Mom said. 'Now back off.'

I shut up. Honestly, it was like being in charge of two listless employees. I was constantly trying to get them to do their best work, but all they did was phone it in.

If they had been employees, I would have fired them a long time ago.

Half an hour later Mom had left for her volunteer shift at the Feline Rescue Association and I was in my room, watching cat videos on YouTube. There was a bunch of new ones, posted under *Purrfect Pet Food's Purrfect Cat Video Contest*. Some of them were mildly amusing, but I could barely concentrate. The voice in my head was getting louder.

Did last night mean something? Does Jacob like me the way I like him? Who am I kidding? As if a guy like him would be interested in me! OH GOD, I'M AN IDIOT!

And on it went.

Just when I'd convinced myself that I would never hear from him again, my phone dinged.

Jacob.

Editing Ivan's video. Want to help?

I didn't hesitate.

Yes.

OK, so we didn't work on the video. We didn't discuss the video. We didn't even use the word *video.*

Jacob's parents had gone to the art gallery. He pulled me into the apartment and down the hall to his room, leaving the door ajar. We collapsed onto his bed.

This time we did more than just kiss.

I could not get enough of him. He slipped his real hand under my top and I slipped a hand under his.

Then we heard the front door open, and his parents hollering out hello.

I practically somersaulted off his bed.

Later that evening I powered up my computer and saw that I had a Facebook notification. I hadn't been on

Facebook in ages, because what was the point? I had about four friends, and two were my mom and dad.

It was a friend request, from K. Apostolos. It took me a minute to realise it was Koula.

I accepted, feeling oddly pleased. Then an ambitious thought struck me: maybe I could up my Facebook friends to the high single digits. I searched for Alonzo Perez and Ivan Bogdanovich and friend requested them, too. Then I searched for Jacob.

A whole pile of Jacob Cohens came up. There were engineering student Jacob Cohens, doctor and lawyer Jacob Cohens, plumber Jacob Cohens, even two city councillor Jacob Cohens. But none of them were *my* Jacob Cohen. I looked on Twitter, Instagram, Tumblr; I couldn't find him anywhere. For a guy who wanted to be a director, he kept an awfully low profile on social media.

Eventually I climbed into bed, Moominmamma and Stuart Little at my feet. I kissed Maxine's photo. I tried to read, but my mind kept wandering to Jacob, and the feel of his hands, the real and the bionic, on my body.

My hand slipped under the covers, down to the waistband of my granny pants. With my other hand, I turned off the light.

TWENTY-ONE

'Write an essay on *The Cellist of Sarajevo*,' Mr Herbert said at the end of English class on Monday. 'I've given you five themes to choose from in the handout.' Clearly he'd given up on thinking outside the box. The bell rang. 'Your marks from the previous assignment are now posted online.'

We left class. Jacob pulled out his phone to look up our mark. Rachel came out after us. 'What did you guys get?' she asked.

Jacob's expression darkened. 'B minus.'

'That's ridiculous. You deserved an A.' Then she headed up the stairs with her newer, shinier friends. Honestly, these brief encounters we were having just left me anxious and confused.

Jacob and I continued down the hall. 'Herbert's a dick,' he said.

'He is.' I liked that we were united in our indignation.

'Our video is better than a lot of the crap on YouTube.'

'Definitely.' That's when it hit me. 'Jacob, we should enter our video in the contest.'

'What contest?'

'I saw it on YouTube yesterday. Purrfect Pet Food is running a contest for best cat video.'

'No.'

'Even if we didn't win, the video would get a lot of exposure.'

'I don't want it posted on YouTube.'

'Herbert would have conniptions if we got a tonne of hits—'

Jacob grabbed my arm with his real hand. 'I don't want it posted online, Petula. OK?'

His grip hurt. 'OK,' I said. 'And, ow.'

Jacob let go. 'Sorry. It's just how I want it.'

'But why?'

He struggled to explain. 'I don't want every single thing I make put out there for the world to see. Does that make sense?'

'Sort of. I guess.' *But not really.*

His shoulders relaxed. 'Thank you.'

Then he leaned in and kissed me.

On the lips.

In the middle of the hall.

Whatever was going on between us, he'd just made it public.

It only lasted a few seconds, but it was long enough for Koula to walk past and shout, 'Get a room!'

TWENTY-TWO

Betty turned up the lights. She'd just watched Jacob's video of our memorial for Ivan's mom. 'What can I say? It's wonderful.'

Jacob's lips curled up in a grin. I squeezed his real hand under the table. He'd finished editing the video a couple of days earlier, and he'd invited all of us – minus Betty – to a private screening at his place. Miranda laid out awesome snacks, like Walkers shortbread biscuits and tortilla chips with homemade guacamole, which I didn't get to try because Koula immediately double-dipped.

We'd watched the video three times in a row. It was fantastic. Through his editing, Jacob had managed to create an actual story. He'd added a moving soundtrack.

Ivan loved it. Even though he was eulogising his dead mom, he was tickled to see himself on Jacob's enormous flat-screen TV. 'I feel like a movie star.'

For YART, Jacob had cut out the fence climbing, the security guard, and the chase sequence. 'Betty gets the Disney version,' he'd told us.

'Ivan, what was it like for you, being able to say goodbye to your mom in your own words?' Betty asked.

'It felt good. I mean, it was sad. But, I don't know, it was also nice, being there with all my friends.'

'I think that's the first time I've heard any of you refer to the others in the group as friends.' Betty smiled. 'We are witnessing something beautiful here. Art truly can be a healing experience.'

Safely out of Betty's line of vision, Koula caught my eye and pretended to vomit.

'You've proved that you're more than capable of generating your own ideas, so you're welcome to do something along these lines again if you want.'

We looked at each other; we hadn't thought that far ahead.

'Or,' Betty continued, opening up her folder, 'I have something fun. We can all draw ourselves as spirit animals—'

'No!' we collectively said.

Alonzo tentatively raised his hand. 'I have an idea for another video.'

'Yes?'

'Remember that movement class I told you guys about?'

'Yeah, that you're weirdly secretive about and that isn't a dance class,' said Koula. 'What kind of movement class is it? Bowel?'

Ivan snorted.

'I haven't wanted to get specific because I assumed some people might poke fun.' Alonzo stared hard at Koula.

'We won't poke fun,' Betty said, looking at the rest of us. 'Right?'

We all nodded, including Koula.

'OK.' Alonzo took a deep breath. 'I've been studying the art of mime.'

Koula burst out laughing. 'Har-har-har-har-har-har. Right.'

'I'm serious. A few years ago I came across the work of Marcel Marceau, the most famous mime ever. And I got hooked.' Alonzo's face grew red as he tried to explain. 'Marceau had a hard life. He was in the French Resistance. His dad was murdered in Auschwitz. But he didn't let any of that break him. He pursued his passion. He could make people laugh one minute, cry the next, and all without saying a word.

'I know it sounds weird, but when I'm miming – it's like I've never felt more like *me*. I can forget about all the noise in my head . . . I feel liberated.'

Koula snorted. Alonzo ignored her.

'I'm getting pretty good. And I've been trying to build up the courage to take it to the streets, to busk.' He turned to Jacob. 'I was thinking we could film it. It would help me see what I'm doing well and what I need to work on. And if it's not awful, maybe I can send a copy of the video to my family.'

'Sure thing,' said Jacob.

Koula crossed her arms over her chest, pouting. 'I can't believe you didn't tell me. Douche bag.'

'Koula, don't make me get the Jar,' said Betty.

'Sorry,' said Alonzo. 'I figured you'd make fun of me.'

'I totally would have. And I totally still will!' Koula started pretending that she was trapped inside a box. Pretty soon we were all doing the same thing, and Betty made us all put a quarter in the Jar.

We gathered on the plaza outside the Vancouver Art Gallery a week later. Koula had painted Alonzo's face to look like a Pierrot doll, complete with white pancake foundation, black eyeliner, and bright red lips. I'd sewn him a Marcel Marceau–like costume, a black-and-white striped T-shirt and black leggings.

While Jacob and Alonzo set up, Ivan bought us lunch with the money we'd pooled. Koula and I sat on the gallery steps. She was sporting a new hairdo. Gone was her big eighties hair, except for a strip down the middle, which she'd dyed bright red and spiked up with gel. It looked oddly appropriate on Koula. She got a lot of looks from passersby, and sitting next to her I felt cool by association.

A handful of people stopped to watch when Alonzo began his performance. First he pretended he was in a slowly shrinking box and couldn't get out. Jacob made him do it again and again so he could shoot it from different angles.

Next, Alonzo mimed that he was having a tug-of-war with an invisible opponent.

'He's good,' I said. 'If you're into mime.'

'Which no one is,' Koula said. 'Except maybe the French. But the French also like Jerry Lewis.'

'You're still miffed that he didn't tell you.'

'Of course I'm miffed. Alonzo and I are not supposed to have secrets. Not if we're going to get married.'

My eyebrows shot up. 'Sorry, what?'

'We've made a deal. If we're both single or divorced or widowed when we're seventy, we're going to marry each other.'

'Oh. Interesting plan.' Koula jiggled her leg up and down. 'How are you doing?'

She shrugged. 'OK. I go to meetings every day. Almost up to my stupid one-month chip again.' She bent over to tie her shoes and I got a close-up of her tattoo.

'Um. About your tattoo.'

'Yeah, yeah, I know. Not one but two spelling mistakes. I had a crazy night with a tattoo artist. We were both wasted. And spelling wasn't his strong point.'

'Can you get it removed?'

'I'm saving up.'

We turned our attention back to Alonzo; he was pretending to walk up a down escalator.

Ivan returned, carrying bags of food from Five Guys. 'Here you go.' He handed Koula and me each a burger and a big carton of fries.

Koula opened the wrapper and took a huge bite. She glanced over at me. 'Tell me you're going to eat that.'

I had not eaten ground beef in two years. Breeding ground for *E. coli* and all that.

But I was starving. And it smelled so good. I took a tentative bite. Then another. It was greasy, salty, and delicious.

Koula was only halfway through her burger by the time I'd finished mine. Which gave me ample time to pour a bunch of fries onto my burger wrapper before she dug her hand in and contaminated them all.

TWENTY-THREE

Something was shifting in me. I woke up in the mornings and actually looked forward to the day. It was such a new feeling that I sometimes thought I'd spontaneously combust, and all that would be left of me was a small pile of ashes next to a smouldering cat hat.

Jacob and I spent a lot of time together. We weren't disgustingly inseparable at school, like Pablo and Carrie, who tongued and groped each other *even on their groinage area* and who looked like conjoined twins when they walked down the halls. But we hung out, a lot. We talked, a lot.

We made out, a lot.

I finished Jacob's dog hat, and it spurred me to do more.

I knitted animal toques for everyone in YART: a monkey for Ivan, a rabbit for Alonzo, and a bear for Betty. For Koula, I made a raccoon headband-style ear warmer so it wouldn't mess up her Mohawk. 'That is so dorky,' she said when I gave it to her. But she wore it. Every day.

I also made a T-shirt tote bag for Rachel. The two of us had taken baby steps; she'd even invited me to eat lunch in the cafeteria with her and her new friends a couple of times. But that was about it.

I still missed her, a lot.

One day Mr Watley stopped me in the hall. 'Petula. How are you doing?'

'Fine. Why?'

'I haven't seen you in my office in weeks.'

'Wow. You're right.'

'So things are good?'

I nodded. 'You'll never guess what I did last week.'

'What?'

'Ate a hamburger.'

'Good for you.'

'And I crossed on a red light. At a very, very quiet intersection in a residential neighbourhood.'

'Goodness! Next you'll be telling me you drank out of a water fountain.'

'Let's not go overboard, sir.'

'I'm glad to hear you're doing well.' Mr Watley gazed at me with his big, watery eyes, and I wondered if he missed me.

'I'm happy to drop by your office once in a while if you'd like,' I said. 'I could even come by today, at lunch—'

'No, no, no need. Just pleased to know you're doing well.' He hurried away, like he'd just farted and didn't want to be around to take the blame when it started to smell.

My mom noticed changes in me, too.

We were eating homemade pizza in front of the TV one night, just the eight of us – two humans, six cats. 'So,' she said out of the blue, 'tell me about you and Jacob.'

'What about me and Jacob?'

'Are you two going steady?'

'Mom, *nobody* says that any more.'

'You know what I mean.'

I shrugged. 'I guess we are.'

'Well, I'm glad. I like him.'

I turned my attention back to the TV.

'If you ever need to talk about anything—'

'Thanks. I'm good.'

'For example, protection and birth control—'

'Mom!'

'I'm just saying, if it ever comes to that, you want to double up, condoms *and* the pill, no unwanted pregnancies, no STIs—'

I upped the volume by ten.

But here's the thing. Since Maxine's death, we hadn't had a lot of genuine mother-daughter conversations.

So even though I'd drowned her out, I was still deeply touched.

She was acting like my mom again.

TWENTY-FOUR

One morning I was flipping through the events section of the paper when something caught my eye. 'Oh my God. Oh. My. God!'

I grabbed the phone to call Rachel.

Then I remembered.

While we were walking to school, I told Jacob about what I'd seen, and how I wished I could invite Rachel. He wore his dog hat and I wore my cat hat. It was sunny and mild; cherry blossoms were starting to bud on the trees. 'So do it. Just ask her,' he said. 'What's the worst that can happen?'

I tried to conjure up something terrible. But the worst I could come up with was 'She says no?' I turned left to avoid the construction site.

'Exactly. It's not life or death. And neither is this.' He didn't turn left. 'Come on, Petula. Walk with me.'

'No.'

'You can do this. Just like you can talk to Rachel.' He reached for my hand. 'We'll do it together. If you want, you can close your eyes.'

My breath started coming in short, sharp bursts.

'Breathe in,' he said. 'Breathe out.'

I did. Then I took his hand and closed my eyes. I leaned into him. I focused on the sounds. Cars. A child wailing. The cries of seagulls overhead.

'There,' Jacob said.

I opened my eyes. We were on the other side of the construction site. He smiled at me. 'See? You are much more capable than you think.' He started to walk again, but I held him back.

Gripping his hand, I turned and made us walk past the construction site again.

On the third time past, I kept my eyes open.

I caught up with Rachel at lunchtime. My palms were moist and my heart was racing, like I was about to ask my crush to the prom. 'There's a huge craft fair at the convention centre this weekend.' Beads of sweat formed on my upper lip. 'Guess who's going to be there.'

Rachel's eyes widened. 'No.'

'Yes. She's doing a demo. I was wondering if you'd like to go.'

Rachel started to laugh. 'Are you kidding? I'm in.'

The convention centre was crowded with fellow craft lovers. Rachel and I wandered up and down the aisles, our heads practically exploding with new ideas. I barely gave a second thought to the germs, the lax security, or the fact that there weren't enough fire exits.

'We have *got* to design our own lampshades,' Rachel said at one point, and my heart soared because she had said *we*.

Just before noon we found seats in front of a makeshift stage at one end of the enormous space. Our crafting idol, Wendy Russell, stepped out to a warm round of applause. Rachel and I spontaneously leapt to our feet. I think we even screamed just a little, seeing her in the flesh.

Wendy wore a shimmery white blouse and jeans with red cowboy boots. Her accessories – a large butterfly brooch and multicoloured cufflets – were her own creations. We knew, because we'd seen her make them on TV.

She gave a demo on how to create a DIY earring holder from an old cheese grater. Rachel and I took notes.

When it was over, Rachel and I moved to the lip of

the stage. Wendy was packing up her supplies. She smiled when she saw us. 'Hi, girls. Did you enjoy the demo?'

We both nodded. 'We're your biggest fans,' said Rachel, her voice quivering.

'That's so nice to hear. You like to craft?'

'We're crafting fiends,' I said. Then I started to giggle uncontrollably, which made Rachel giggle, too.

'Can we have your autograph?' asked Rachel.

'Of course.' Wendy signed our craft fair programmes. Then she reached into her supply kit and handed us each a bottle of high-quality fabric paint. 'It was a pleasure meeting you both.' She held out her bare hand. And I shook it.

When she was gone, I didn't take out my bottle of sanitiser. I didn't run to the bathroom to wash my hands through two rounds of 'Happy Birthday'. Because whatever germs Wendy Russell had, they were Wendy Russell germs, and I wanted as much of her to rub off on me as possible.

Rachel and I were buzzing with excitement when we left the convention centre. 'We *have* to make those earring holders,' said Rachel. 'Like, today.'

I looked at her. 'You mean, together?'

'Yes, dorkus. Together. We just need to buy cheese graters. I have everything else we need at my house.'

Her house.

My bowels clenched.

'Um. I just remembered.'

Her pace slowed. 'Remembered what?'

'This thing. With my mom.'

She stopped. Hands on hips. 'Oh, really? What thing?'

'A movie.'

'What movie?'

'That one. With the dark-haired actress. You know.'

Rachel's tone shifted. 'OK. Whatever.'

'I'm sorry, Rachel.'

'Hey. No worries.' She gave me a sad smile. 'See you Monday.' She walked away.

I wanted to shout at her to come back. I'd missed her so much, and the day had been so awesome, and now it was falling to pieces, all thanks to me.

But seeing her happy, intact family, seeing Owen . . .

I just couldn't do it. In spite of all the steps I'd taken, this one felt enormous, insurmountable. Just the thought of it made me nauseous with anxiety, even though I badly wanted Rachel's friendship again.

So I turned in the other direction. *Stupid you. Stupid, fearful you.*

The gulf between me and my former best friend had finally started closing, and I'd just torn it open again.

TWENTY-FIVE

When I got home, Mom came into the foyer carrying Stuart Little. 'Well? How'd it go with Rachel?'

Tears welled in my eyes. Mom kept the cat in one arm and wrapped her other arm around me, holding me close. 'Oh, Tula. What happened?'

'We had a great time. But she wanted me to come over. And I couldn't face seeing Owen, I just couldn't.' Stuart Little made little *merp* sounds that I'd never heard before; he seemed to enjoy being squashed between us.

I pulled away.

Stuart Little's stripes looked different.

It wasn't Stuart Little.

'Mom. No.'

'Isn't she cute? I've called her Pippi Longstocking because of her white legs—'

'*Mom.*'

'Don't be mad. Angie was—'

'Let me guess, in a pinch—'

'She's five years old, abandoned by her owners to fend for herself or starve to death—'

'We can hardly afford the cats we have! The apartment's not big enough for more!'

Now Mom was getting teary-eyed. 'I know, I know. But what was I supposed to do?'

'Say no! Oh my God, how many cats will it take to make up for one child?'

Mom reeled back like she'd been slapped. '*That* was mean.'

'I'm sorry. I'm sorry, OK? But Dad is going to *freak out.*'

'He already did. He's gone for a walk.'

I shook my head.

'I swear this is temporary. I'm trying my best to get them adopted. So please, don't you be mad at me, too.'

I sighed. 'Not mad.'

'Thank you.' She pulled me close again and we stayed like that for a while, the new cat *merping* happily between us.

That night in my room I texted off and on with Jacob. Then I watched a few cat videos, including a couple more in *Purrfect Pet Food's Cat Video Contest.*

Ours is so much better, I thought.

I clicked through to Purrfect Pet Food's site. That's where I read that the grand prize was a lifetime supply of cat food.

A lifetime supply of cat food.

My parents wouldn't have to worry about the cost of feeding so many cats. It would be one less thing for them to argue about.

We, of all people, could really use that prize.

I hesitated for only a moment.

Then I found the USB stick Jacob had given me.

Ten minutes later, I'd entered *Wuthering Heights: A Cataptation* into the contest.

I decided not to tell Jacob what I'd done. Chances were good that nothing would happen.

He'd probably never find out.

TWENTY-SIX

Koula's house was practically mansion-sized, a big white stucco place at Fraser and the Kingsway. In front was a well-maintained garden.

I'm not sure what I'd expected. Not this.

'I grew up here,' she told us as we approached from the bus stop. 'When my folks split, I lived with my mom in Kitsilano. But she kicked me out over a year ago, so I moved back in with my dad.'

The five of us headed through the wrought iron gate. Rosebushes, carefully wrapped in burlap for the winter, lined the walkway. Koula opened the door and we stepped into a large foyer. 'Take your shoes off,' she told us, then yelled something in Greek before leading us into a big kitchen.

A man was at the table, drinking coffee and reading a Greek newspaper. He had white hair and bushy eyebrows and a stern look on his face. I assumed it was her grandpa until she said, 'Everyone, this is my dad.'

Having a daughter like Koula had probably aged him.

Mr Apostolos spoke sharply in Greek. She answered in English. 'Relax, *Bampas*. They're not druggies, they're friends from art class. We're here to shoot a video.'

Betty had loved Alonzo's piece. Jacob had done an amazing job yet again, managing to make the film both funny and poignant. Edith Piaf's *'Non, Je Ne Regrette Rien'* played throughout. Alonzo loved it, too. He'd sent a copy to his family.

Koula and I had both come up with ideas for videos, too. The only one who hadn't come up with an idea was Jacob. 'I don't need to,' he'd argued in YART. 'Directing them is my therapy.' I could see that, in a way, this was true. He looked so at ease, so content when he was behind the camera.

Koula's dad still eyed us with suspicion. Jacob pulled off his John Deere cap and stuck out his bionic hand. 'It's nice to meet you, sir.'

Mr Apostolos immediately brightened. 'That's a beauty,' he said as he shook it. 'I work in biotechnology.'

The ice was broken. Koula's dad insisted on giving us

snacks of dolmas, pita, and hummus while he talked to Jacob about his prosthetic limb. Ivan shovelled down most of the food; I wondered if his dad ever fed him.

Finally Koula said, 'Stop talking his ear off, *Bampas*! We have work to do.'

We followed Koula upstairs, to her bedroom. 'Nobody laugh.' She pushed open the door.

It was pink. Pink walls, pink frilly bedspread, pink area rug, pink curtains. A shelf above a white desk – the only non-pink piece of furniture in the room – held a bunch of trophies. Shot-putting? Rugby? I studied the hardware more closely. 'You were on *Reach for the Top*?' I couldn't keep the surprise out of my voice. *Reach for the Top* is like a sports event for the brainy set, where schools compete against each other to see who has the most knowledge. Sort of like *Jeopardy!* but without the cash prizes.

'Yep. At Trafalgar Secondary.'

Alonzo flopped onto Koula's bed. 'Hard as it is to believe, she's kind of a brainiac.'

Jacob put his lucky director's cap back on and started setting up.

Koula's idea was simple, based on some other videos she'd seen. She'd written out short sentences in black Magic Marker on a series of index cards. The statements were her version of making amends.

Jacob put his camera on a tripod. 'Koula, you have to be a hundred per cent on your game. We have to shoot it in one take.'

'Got it. I've been rehearsing a lot.'

'OK, then. You ready?'

'Ready.'

Jacob started recording. Ivan stood briefly in front of the camera. 'Koula video, take one.'

'Action.'

Koula looked directly into the camera and held up the cards one by one.

My name is Koula.

I am an addict.

I've been clean four weeks, five days, and thirteen hours.

Not that I'm counting.

I started using three years ago.

Whatever pills I found in the medicine cabinet.

It snowballed from there.

I wish I could tell you the reason.

There was no creepy uncle.

No abusive parents.

Nobody died.

The truth is, I liked it.

But pretty soon I couldn't stop.

Koula paused before she held up the next card.

I used to have good friends.
I lost them.
I used to have parents who trusted me.
I lost that trust.
I don't expect to get my friends back.
But I want to say I'm sorry.
Sorry for the lousy things I did when I was high.
Sorry for the lousy things I did to get high.
Alberta, I'm sorry I stole twenty bucks from your purse.
Twice.
Parvana, I'm sorry I stole the charm bracelet Ambrose
gave you.
Henry and Farley, I'm sorry I stole a bunch of your
recycling money.
Sheri, I'm sorry I punched you. I thought you were
hitting on Braeden.
You were hitting on Braeden.
But still. That's no excuse.
Carol Polachuk, I'm sorry I shit on your desk.

'You WHAT?' Alonzo shrieked, blowing the take. Ivan burst out laughing.

Jacob stopped recording. Koula looked at the card. 'Oh, for— No, I didn't shit on her desk. I *put* shit on her desk.'

'*Yours?*' I asked.

'Of course not! Gross!' Koula tried to explain. 'She was

making me crazy, OK? I didn't want to see her any more. So I got high outside, before one of our sessions. This woman walked by with her dog, and it took a dump on the grass, right in front of me. The woman scooped it into a bag and started looking around for a garbage can. And I said, "There's a bin near the front entrance. I'll take it for you." But instead of throwing it in the garbage, I emptied it onto Carol's desk. It made infinite sense at the time.'

Koula rewrote the card. Once we'd all stopped laughing, Jacob filmed again from the top. On the fifth attempt, Koula got all the way through to the end.

Last but not least, to my parents.

Mom and Dad, I will spend the rest of my life . . .

. . . trying to make amends for the crap I put you through.

All the stuff I stole.

All the nights I didn't come home.

All the lies I told.

Dad, thanks for letting me back in your life.

I'll try not to let you down.

Mom, I understand why you haven't let me back in yet.

Maybe, in a few more months, we can try again.

And finally . . .

... please consider donating to my Kickstarter campaign ...

She turned around. Jacob zoomed in on her BEATIFUL TRADGEDY tattoo. After a few moments Koula turned back to face the camera and held up her last two cards.

So I can get this removed.

Any amount would be greatly appreciated.

TWENTY-SEVEN

Jacob invited me over after we'd wrapped. I was happy to accept, because the tension at my house was thick. Dad was still furious about Pippi Longstocking.

'We're not an animal shelter. The apartment smells!'

'It's temporary!'

'So you keep saying, and nothing happens.'

It had been like that all week, the same arguments over and over. When I told Jacob, he'd said, 'Sounds like the movie *Groundhog Day*. Without the laughs.'

His parents were out for the evening and wouldn't be home until late. We ordered a pizza and watched one of Jacob's favourite movies, *Moonrise Kingdom*.

'I love this film,' Jacob said when it was over. 'Wes

Anderson is a genius. I wish I could live in this film.' He stared at the screen, watching the credits roll. 'You ever wish your life was more like a movie?'

'I've never really thought about it.'

'I think about it all the time. You could choose what story to tell. You could set the tone. You could direct the whole thing. You could edit out the crappy parts.'

'That would be nice.'

'Better still, you could do a page-one rewrite.'

'I'd like that.' Maxine would still be alive in mine. Jacob would still have Randle and Ben. A thought struck me. 'If we rewrote our lives, you and I might never meet.'

'Sure we would. I'd make mine a rom-com. We'd meet by chance somewhere. Like sitting next to each other on a plane.'

'Except I will never set foot on a plane.' I started to reel off a list of aviation disasters, but then Jacob shut me up by putting his lips on mine.

We kissed all the way down the hall to his bedroom. He left the door open a crack. 'What about your parents?'

'I'll hear them if they come in. And they won't be back for hours.'

Things heated up, fast. His window literally got steamy.

We'd fooled around a lot, but we always kept our clothes on.

Until now.

I unbuttoned his shirt and tugged it off. He carefully pulled my bleach-art T-shirt over my head.

Soon our jeans were on the floor. I had a moment of panic when I realised I was wearing my old granny underwear. When I'd put it on I'd had no idea that this was where the day would take me.

But Jacob gazed at scrawny me in my saggy pants, my functional beige bra, and hand-knit toe socks, and said, 'You're beautiful.'

I wanted to weep. I gazed back at him in his black boxer briefs and the shark socks I'd recently knitted for him, which made it look like the sharks were eating his feet. His skin was so pale, it was almost translucent. 'So are you.'

Then he said the magic words that took our relationship to a whole new level.

'Do you want to see my stump?'

It was the most romantic thing anyone had ever said to me.

He carefully unstrapped his artificial limb and placed it on the night table. I gently ran my fingers along the stub of what was left of his arm. It freaked me out at first;

it was lumpy with scar tissue and, well . . . stumpy. But I knew it was a big deal that he'd shown me. 'Thank you.'

Jacob drew a heart in the steam on his window and added our initials to it. We crawled under the bedcovers and faced each other, naked except for our socks and undies. Our noses touched.

'I think I love you, Petula.'

I was glad I was lying down, because I suddenly felt dizzy and off-kilter, like I used to before I was about to faint. 'I think I love you, too.'

Words I never thought I would say, except to my parents.

Words I never thought anyone would say to me, except for my parents.

Words I didn't think I'd ever deserve to hear.

We started kissing again. I slid off his underwear. He slid off mine.

'Are we doing what I think we're doing?' he asked.

'I'd like to give it a try.'

'Have you ever . . . ?'

'*Pssh,* what do you think? Of course not. You?'

'No.'

'We have to be safe.'

'Definitely. No teen pregnancies on our watch.'

I was thinking of much more than that. But I didn't

want to spoil the mood by telling Jacob everything I'd read about pubic lice, crabs, genital warts, venereal disease, HIV, syphilis, and more.

'I have condoms,' he said. 'My uncle gave me a box of them for Hanukkah, mostly to bug my parents. He called it a preemptive strike.'

He leapt out of bed, naked except for the shark socks, and got the box of condoms from his desk drawer. Then he crawled back under the covers and pulled out one of the packets. 'I've never put one on before.'

'Me neither. But I've stuffed a lot of sock monkeys.'

He winced. 'That does not inspire confidence.'

'I also saw a demo once in health class, with a cucumber.'

'Better.'

'Let's make it a team effort.'

I took the packet out of his hand and tore it open.

In a movie, this is where the script would read:

Fade to black.

TWENTY-EIGHT

I told my mom a few days later.

Well, I didn't tell her, exactly. I wrote her a note.

Dad was working late and we were eating dinner in front of the TV again.

Re: Our earlier conversation, the note read. *I think I need to see our family doctor and go on the pill.*

Mom read it. Her eyes filled with tears. A couple of them plopped onto her spaghetti.

After a moment she picked up the pen and wrote. She passed the paper back to me. *Thank you for telling me. Would you like me to come with you?*

I wrote, *Yes.*

Mom booked me an appointment with our family

doctor. Jacob offered to come, but I wanted to go with my mom.

We caught a bus to Dr Bahri's office in Kitsilano. She was very kind, yet it didn't make having the insertion of a cold metal object into my lady parts any more pleasant. But this was the cost of doing business, and I wanted to do business.

After the appointment Mom and I walked down Broadway together. I was sure I was walking funny.

'How do you feel?'

'Like aliens just beamed me into their spaceship and probed my orifices.'

'She only probed one orifice.'

'Actually, three. She also checked my ears for wax build-up.'

We stopped at Kidsbooks, which was Mom's favourite bookstore and the one she hoped to work at one day if a full-time position opened up. Then we walked to Dairy Queen. 'Backwards dinner?' asked Mom. We used to do backwards dinner a couple of times a year when Maxine was still alive, eating dessert first, the main course second.

'Most definitely yes.'

Mom took my hand and we went inside. She ordered us each a Peanut Buster Parfait. As we both shovelled deliciousness into our mouths, she said, 'Just remember, Petula. It's all about mutual respect. You must always be kind and thoughtful and honest with each other.'

Kind, thoughtful, honest.

I was sure Jacob and I had all three covered.

TWENTY-NINE

Something else happened during those weeks.

I allowed optimism to creep in.

Optimists believe things will always work out for the best. Optimists live in a rainbow-coloured, sugar-coated land of denial.

Optimists miss warning signs.

Like the Saturday morning I was over at Jacob's place, sitting on his bed and knitting while he edited Koula's video.

He stood up and stretched. 'I'm starving. Want a sandwich? PB and J?'

'Sure.' His parents always bought bread and jams from

the farmers' market, so even the most basic of sandwiches was elevated to a whole new level of delicious.

My fingers needed a rest, so I put my knitting needles down and wandered around his room. I wasn't snooping, not exactly. But when I found his old high school yearbook wedged behind other books on his shelf, I was immediately intrigued. NORTHWESTERN SECONDARY was on the cover in embossed gold lettering. There was so little personal stuff in Jacob's room, this small discovery felt huge.

I found his class photo. *Goal: To become the next Steven Spielberg.* Then I searched for the senior boys' basketball team photo. Jacob was in the back row. I was about to read the names in the caption to see if I could find Randle and Ben when something fluttered out from between the pages.

It was a blue envelope, addressed to Jacob. The return address read *S. Esterhasz.*

Suddenly a bionic hand slammed the book shut, scaring the crap out of me. 'You shouldn't snoop,' Jacob said.

'Says the guy who read my scrapbook when I first met him. You practically gave me a heart attack.'

He took the yearbook out of my hands and put it back on the shelf. Then he crumpled the envelope into a ball and stuffed it into his pocket.

'Letter from an old girlfriend?' I asked. Only half-joking.
He said nothing.

'You never talk about your friends. It's OK to talk about
them, Jacob. You let me talk about Maxine. I like talking
about Maxine.'

'Yeah, well. We're different that way.' He sat beside me
on the bed. 'I'm sorry. I didn't mean to startle you. And
I never mind when you talk about Maxine. I'm just— It's
not who I am.'

Then he started to kiss me. Which led to the inevitable.
And I forgot all about the momentary weirdness.

There was also the Sunday night in March, when Jacob
invited everyone from YART to come over and watch
Inglourious Basterds, another of his favourites. It was
getting dark out, and we could see the lights from the
tankers that were always moored in English Bay, part
creepy, part beautiful.

Miranda laid out more awesome snacks: chips, smelly
cheeses, strawberries that tasted like strawberries even
though they weren't in season. I made myself a heaping
plate before Koula started double-dipping.

Koula and Alonzo sprawled out on the couch, one of
them at each end, feet touching. Jacob, Ivan, and I
propped ourselves up with cushions on the rug.

The movie was fantastic. Normally I couldn't take that much violence, but when it involved a successful plot to assassinate Hitler, even I had to get on board. Jacob gave a running commentary about the techniques Quentin Tarantino had used, until Koula yelled, 'Oh my God, shut *up*!'

'I modelled my first films after Tarantino,' Jacob said when the movie was finished.

'Really? Can we see one?' Ivan spoke through a mouthful of chips.

Jacob shook his head.

'Come on, we won't judge,' said Koula.

'Yes, you will,' he said to her. 'You judge everything.'

'Maybe so. But I also confessed my worst sins in front of all of you. And there's no way your early films are more embarrassing than *miming in public.*'

Alonzo kicked her. 'Thank you, Koula. Thank you so much.'

'She's kind of right, though.' Bits of chip sprayed onto the carpet as Ivan spoke. 'We've told you a lot.'

'We've pretty much bared our souls to you,' said Koula. 'And I bet Petula's bared more than that.' She and Alonzo laughed, and I felt my face go hot.

They kept pestering him, and Jacob finally said, 'Fine. One. I'll show you one.' He hooked his laptop up to the flat-screen TV. He found the file he was looking for and hit Play.

It was five minutes long. The premise: A constipated burglar breaks into a house. He suddenly feels like he has to go. He leaves his gun outside the bathroom. The owner comes home while the burglar is straining to go. He picks up the burglar's gun and kills him in a hail of bullets while the burglar is still sitting on the toilet. The burglar's last words as he lies dying in a pool of blood: 'On the bright side . . . I pooped.'

It was juvenile and over the top, but we still laughed.

Except for Jacob. He didn't even watch it. He unhooked his laptop before the credits could roll.

Ivan figured it out before the rest of us. 'The two actors. They were your friends, weren't they? The ones who died.'

Jacob didn't respond.

'Do you feel guilty?' asked Koula.

He gave her a sharp look. 'About what?'

'That you lived, and they didn't?'

'Every day.'

'You shouldn't. It's wasted energy.'

'But we all feel that way, don't we?' said Alonzo. 'Guilty.'

'What do you feel guilty for?' asked Koula. 'Loving mime?'

'No, bitchy-poo. Being gay.'

Koula groaned. 'Oh, get over it.'

'It's not that easy. My whole life I've been told it's a sin. It's hard to shake that stuff.'

'I feel guilty, too,' I said. 'It may not be rational, but it doesn't mean you don't feel it anyway.'

'I sometimes think,' said Ivan, 'if I hadn't made my mom mad? She never would have swum out so far.' Tears started to roll down his face.

Jacob put an arm around Ivan. 'What happened to your mom was not your fault.' He glared at the rest of us. 'This conversation is over.'

Alonzo shrugged. 'If we can't have this conversation with each other, who can we have it with?'

He had a point.

Jacob wasn't in school the following morning.

He didn't come to school for three whole days.

And last but not least: a couple of weeks later, Serge the Concierge stopped me as I entered the lobby and asked if I'd bring a letter up to the Cohens. 'It got placed in the wrong mailbox.'

It was another thin blue envelope, addressed to Jacob. The return address: S. Esterhasz. I held the envelope under the light in the stairwell as I walked up to the sixth floor, but I couldn't read anything.

Miranda opened the door. 'Serge asked me to bring this up.' I handed her the letter.

The colour drained from her face. She took the letter from me. 'Thank you. I'll give it to him later.' I kicked off my shoes and started towards Jacob's room. 'Oh, and Petula? If you wouldn't mind, don't mention this to him, OK?'

That seemed weird. But I said nothing.

The next day Jacob wasn't in school, again. He didn't respond to my texts. His mom answered when I called their house; she said simply that he was 'under the weather.'

I was pretty sure that was code for 'depressed'. Every single one of us in YART had gone down that rabbit hole, and more than once.

I worried about Jacob when he dropped out like that, but after a couple of days he'd resurface and be his usual cheerful self.

It's only with hindsight that I see those moments were clues to something bigger. And that's the downside of optimism.

It makes you blind to signs of trouble ahead.

THIRTY

'You either need way more streamers or none at all,' said Koula. She lay on the couch. Pippi Longstocking was on her chest, purring loudly.

I was on a stepladder, trying to tape streamers to the ceiling. 'It might look better if I had some help.'

She didn't budge. 'I feel I'm best in a supervisory role.'

My parents' anniversary wasn't for four more days, but I was surprising them early. At first I'd had more than enough helpers, but they'd dropped out one by one. Ivan's dad had offered to take him go-karting, which was a huge breakthrough. 'We haven't done anything fun together since Mom died,' Ivan told us. Jacob's parents had surprised him with a ski weekend in

Whistler. And Alonzo had recently met a boy in his movement class; he bailed at the last minute to spend the day with him.

'Do you actually make out?' Koula had asked him the day before at YART. 'Or do you just mime making out?' Her bitterness was putting a strain on their friendship.

So it was just me and Koula. It was the first time she'd been to my house. I'd been worried she'd make fun of all the cats. But she loved them, especially Pippi. 'Look at her,' she said now as Pippi kneaded her paws into Koula's chest. 'She loves me!' She talked to the cat in a baby voice. 'Who's da pwetty kitty? Who's da pwetty kitty?'

I gave up on the streamers and ran into the kitchen to check on the cake.

I'd gotten my parents out of the house with a gift certificate for a couple's massage at a downtown spa. It had cost a small fortune, emptying what was left of my bank account. But it was worth it.

When I came back into the living room, Koula was rubbing noses with Pippi. 'So,' she said. 'Are you and Jacob . . .' She made an obscene gesture with her hands.

'That is really none of your business.'

'So, yes.'

I didn't answer.

'Whatever. If you are, I'm going to assume it's nice. For both of you. Doing it with someone you actually, you know, care about.'

'So, you've . . . ?'

'Sure. Couple I remember. Couple I don't.'

'That sucks, Koula.'

'Yeah. Well.' She rubbed Pippi's belly. 'Anyway. I'm glad for you. Jacob's a good guy. Even if he is kind of mysterious.'

'What do you mean?'

'He never talks about his own crap. You know, his dead friends and everything.'

I shrugged. 'We all deal with things in different ways.'

'Yeah, but we've told him a tonne. He hasn't told us much at all. It's like we've peeled back all our layers, and he's only peeled back maybe one.'

'I think that's your soap operas talking,' I said. I knew Koula watched at least three of them religiously.

Pippi batted at Koula's nose, trying to get her attention. 'You is such a silly kitty,' Koula said in her baby voice.

A thought struck me. 'Does your dad like cats?'

'He's indifferent. Why?'

'Mom's trying to find a forever home for Pippi.'

'Are you serious?'

'Very. You'd be doing us a huge favour. It would be the ultimate anniversary gift.'

'I'll totally take her! But just a heads-up: I'm changing her name.' Koula looked at Pippi. 'From now on, you're Lorena Bobbitt.'

'Who's Lorena Bobbitt?'

Koula punched in the name into Google on her phone and handed it to me.

'Oh, Koula,' I said.

She cackled.

I'd rented a helium tank for the afternoon, and Koula finally got off her butt to help with the balloons. Except she kept taking small sips of helium. 'Do you think your sponsor would approve?' I asked.

'Who cares? This is so much fun!' She sounded like Alvin the Chipmunk.

At four p.m. I took the cake out of the oven. Then I got supper started. I was keeping it simple with a three-step lasagna and salad.

My parents weren't due home for at least another hour. I'd told them I'd be out when they got back. The plan was that I would greet them with a candlelit room and a glass of wine. Then I would show them the video I had made for YART. Afterwards I would serve dinner and leave. Koula had said she'd hang around downtown so we could go see a movie. My parents would have the apartment to themselves for the rest of the night.

So I was startled when I heard a key in the lock.

Koula and I were in the kitchen, where I was icing the cake. Koula, who'd just taken another sip of helium, squeaked, 'Hide!' She slid the door closed.

'I just wanted to have a relaxing cup of tea after the massage,' I heard Dad say. 'But you had to ruin it by dredging things up—'

'How is it dredging things up to talk about our daughter?'

'You do it all the time.'

'I don't do it all the time! You make me feel like I can't. It's awful, not being able to talk about Maxine when I want to.'

'I'm sorry. But you have to respect my way of dealing with things—'

'Which is to act like she didn't exist—'

'She does exist!' Dad was shouting. 'She exists in every breath I take. Every moment I mourn for her, but I just don't need to talk about her all the goddamn time!' Suddenly there was a screech from one of the cats; he must have stepped on a tail. 'Jesus Christ, are you even *trying* to get these goddamn cats adopted?'

Koula stared at me, wide-eyed.

'Oh God,' my mom said, and I knew they'd stepped into the balloon-strewn living room.

A moment later Dad opened the kitchen door. 'Happy anniversary!' Koula squeaked in her helium voice.

'Hey, I'm Koula, really great to meet you both,' Koula said as she slipped past my stricken parents. She grabbed her Doc Martens from the foyer. 'I'm, uh, I'll just put these on in the hall.' To me, she said, 'How's about I pick up Lorena next weekend?' She slipped out of the apartment, closing the door behind her.

My parents looked ashen. They apologised. I tried my best to regroup. I poured them each a glass of wine and made them sit on the couch. I hooked up Mom's laptop to the TV and put in the USB stick Jacob had given me the night before. 'I have a special present for you.'

My idea had kept us busy at YART for quite a while. I'd pulled boxes of photos and old videos from our storage locker and the five of us had divvied up the work, watching hours of footage and sifting through hundreds of photos, marking the best. Jacob had painstakingly edited the video and added music.

But even as the opening frames came up, I felt an impending sense of doom.

It was ten minutes long. The first part, set to 'I'm a Believer', by the Monkees, was a series of pictures and videos that told the story of how my parents had met. It included footage from university and trips they'd taken, like hiking in the Andes and trekking in Nepal. The second part, set to 'Chapel of Love' by the Dixie Cups, had footage from their wedding day and their honeymoon in Nicaragua.

The last part, set to 'Our House', by Crosby, Stills, Nash, and Young, was about their growing family. It showed Mom nursing me, Dad giving me a bottle, my first steps. School concerts, the three of us skating at Robson Square.

But the bulk of the last segment was about Maxine. At the playground, opening presents on Christmas morning, playing at the beach.

When it was over we were all crying, even my dad.

'That was beautiful, Petula,' Mom said.

'I wanted to show you that you've had a really good life together,' I said.

They glanced at each other.

'What?'

'We were waiting for a good time to tell you,' Dad said.

The dread I'd been feeling since they first walked through the door grew to soccer-ball-size in my stomach.

'Your mom and I decided a while back to have a trial separation,' Dad said.

'Trial,' Mom added. 'Nothing set in stone.'

'That's right. This isn't a divorce. It's a break.'

I didn't stick around to hear any more.

I fast-walked down the street and didn't even realise till I was two blocks away that not only had I forgotten my rape whistle, I'd just crossed at a crosswalk without looking left or right. *That's* how mad I was.

I was furious with them but also with myself. *You've been slacking off around the house for weeks! If only you'd stayed vigilant!*

'Petula!' Dad's voice. I picked up my pace. But Dad is a runner, and he easily caught up with me. He put a hand on my arm.

I turned around and punched him as hard as I could in the chest. My keys were between my knuckles, so it hurt. 'Ow!'

I punched him again before he grabbed my hand, forced open my fingers, and took the keys. 'Stop it. Just stop.' He held my wrists so I wouldn't hit him again. 'I'm sorry you had to find out this way. But, Petula, it's been a long time coming. We've been trying to make this work for a while.'

'Have you? Have you really?'

'Yes. We have.'

'How, exactly? How, exactly, have you tried? By never being home? By spending evenings and weekends at the office?' I was so mad, I was shaking.

'I did my best. *We* did our best. That's why we started seeing the marriage counsellor.' He let go of my wrists and looked up at the night sky. 'You have to believe me when I say that neither of us wanted this to happen. We held on for as long as we could.'

Don't cry, don't cry, said my inner voice.

I started to cry. 'I tried so hard to make things work.'

'Sweetheart. Why should you try to make our marriage work?'

'Because it's all my fault. If I hadn't made that stupid wolf suit, we'd be fine, everything would be fine—'

Dad gripped my shoulders. 'Listen to me. Are you listening? You are not responsible for Maxine's death, or the state of our marriage. Do you understand?' He shook me a little too hard. 'If anyone's to blame, it's me.'

'What are you talking about?'

'Your mom and I were supposed to take Maxine to the new Pixar movie that day. Remember? Instead I saw an ad in the newspaper for a sale at Skip to My Loo, the bath shop. I told Maxine we'd take her another day. When we left the house, she was so upset. That was the last time I saw her alive.' Now my dad was crying, too. 'A new shower curtain and towels. That was my priority. I think about that every day.'

I hadn't remembered any of this. 'Dad, that's ridiculous. It wasn't your fault.'

'I know. On good days, I know. But, Petula, the same holds true for you. You have to believe me when I say it wasn't your fault, either. We've never blamed you.'

That just made me cry even harder.

A couple walking by with their dog stared at us, trying to gauge if I was in any sort of trouble. 'Keep walking!' I shouted.

'I've been a lousy father to you since Maxine died. I know that.'

'Yeah, maybe.'

'I'm going to try to do better from now on.'

'By leaving?'

'Crazy as it sounds, yes. I think your mother and I might do better if we're apart.'

'You used to love each other so much.'

'We still do. But we can't look at each other without remembering, without feeling this tremendous weight of sadness.'

'You might be just as sad apart.'

'Yes.'

'Or sadder.'

'Yes. But that's something we need to find out.' Then Dad did something he hadn't done in a long time.

He pulled me into a hug and held me tight. 'You're the reason we stuck it out for as long as we did, sweetie. You're the reason we almost made it to twenty.'

THIRTY-ONE

Maxine visited me again in my sleep.

We were back in our old apartment. I found her sitting on the living room floor, doing one of her favourite large-piece puzzles. I was flooded with happiness and relief.

But this wasn't cheerful Maxine.

This was full-on tantrum Maxine. When she saw me she launched herself at me, her face beetroot red, her little fists flailing.

'I'm sorry, Max. I'm sorry.' I could hear a *ping* in the background as she hit me. Then she started scratching my face—

I woke up. Heavy rain was pelting the window. Ferdinand was sitting by my head, batting at my nose with his paws. Memories from last night washed over me. Ugh.

Another *ping*. It was my phone.

I had a series of texts from Jacob.

Raining on the mountain.

Heading home early.

You around?

I typed: *Yes. Back when?*

Couple hours. How'd the surprise go?

AWFUL.

So sorry. Home by one. Come over?

OK.

I put down my phone. Anne of Green Gables and Stuart Little were at the end of my bed. I sat up and lifted them onto my stomach. Stanley wandered in and joined the rest of us. They were probably hungry, but they knew they had a job to do, and that was to comfort me.

I lay back down and petted all four of them. Letting myself just be sad.

I was forced to get up an hour later when Ferdinand threw up an enormous hair ball on my duvet. I cleaned it up and made a quick run to the kitchen to feed the cats, grabbing myself two bagels and a banana at the same time. My parents were nowhere to be seen, thank God. I just could not handle seeing them.

I showered. I got dressed. It was still only eleven-thirty. So I went online.

It had been a few weeks since I'd uploaded *Cataptation* to the pet food contest. Last time I'd checked, our video was buried deep among the other entries and had only one hundred and twenty views. I decided to have another look.

I found our video immediately. It was almost at the top.

I had to keep looking at the number. I was sure I was adding an extra zero. But no, the figure was correct.

Forty-two thousand, two hundred fifty-six views.

A lot of people had voted for it. It was currently in third place.

I did a happy dance around my room, almost stepping on yet another of Anne of Green Gables's stealth turds, tucked underneath a pair of my discarded socks.

Serge the Concierge was on the phone when I entered the lobby. He smiled and waved me up.

Miranda answered the door. Her purple glasses magnified her eyes, and it looked like she'd been crying. 'Jacob's in his room. He's— He may not want guests.'

'Oh. He told me to come over.'

She gave a sort of vague nod, and walked with me down the hall. Jacob's door was ajar. He sat at his desk, staring into space.

'Jacob, Petula's here.'

He stood up and smiled. It looked forced. 'Hey.'

'I'll leave you two alone.' Miranda slipped away.

'What's wrong? Are you OK?'

'Yeah, I'm fine. Just tired.' We sat down on his bed. 'Tell me what happened last night.'

'Long story short? They're separating.'

'Petula. I'm so sorry.' He pulled me to him and held me close for a long time, stroking my hair. He was wearing his green sweater, and I felt warm and safe as I breathed him in.

'I need to tell you something,' I said into his sweater.

'Shoot.'

'A couple of weeks ago I entered our *Cataptation* video into that pet food contest.'

He grew still.

I looked up at him. 'I know you asked me not to. But, Jacob, the prize is a lifetime supply of cat food. That would be huge for my family. And get this, it's in third place! We have over forty thousand views.'

His face was a blank.

'Please don't be mad. This is good for you, too. People love it, Jacob. They love your work.'

'Wow.'

'I know, right?'

'I was so clear.' He stood up.

'Jacob. It's a hit.'

'My name is on that film.'

'Exactly. Isn't that the point? Don't you want your work out there?'

He ran his hand through his hair. 'I want you to take it down.'

'What? Why? I don't see what the problem is.'

'Just do it, OK?' I'd never seen him this angry.

But I was angry, too. 'In case you weren't listening, my parents are separating. They already struggle to make ends meet; now they're going to have to pay for two apartments. If I win this contest, I'm saving them at least a hundred bucks a month. So, no. It's my video too, and I won't take it down, especially since you can't even give me a reasonable explanation!'

He stared at me, hard. 'I think you'd better go.'

I stood up. 'Oh, trust me, I'm going. Call me if you decide to stop being a dick.'

As I walked out, I noticed a thin blue envelope sitting open on his desk.

THIRTY-TWO

I was a mess of emotions when I got home. Jacob and I had never fought before. It was like I'd seen an entirely different person. And I didn't like what I'd seen.

My parents forced me to eat dinner with them. I hardly touched my food. They tried to involve me in their discussion about 'next steps'. 'Your dad's going to move out at the end of the month,' Mom said.

'I've rented a place that's very close by,' Dad added. 'You'll have your own room there, too, of course.'

I could barely process their words. They exchanged concerned glances, and when I asked if I could be excused, they said yes.

I didn't know what to do. Should I take down the video? Jacob was so obviously upset.

I went on YouTube and found *Cataptation*. Even if I wanted to delete it, I didn't see how I could. It was part of the contest. It had also been shared a lot.

This time I noticed the comments section.

I scrolled down and read some of them. A few people thought the video was stupid. A few animal rights activists thought it was pet abuse.

But most people thought it was hilarious.

> Do one based on a Dickens novel!
>
> Hope this one wins!
>
> I beg you, do *Lord of the Flies*!!!!!
>
> LOL, this is funnier than Maru!
>
> The Dumbing-Down of North America Continues.

This was written by someone with the username Herbie_the_Love_Bug. I wondered if it was Mr Herbert.

> Is the director the same Jacob S. Cohen who
>
> went to Northwestern Secondary in Toronto?

This was written by a shirlest123. There was an option to respond to the comments, so I replied with my username, which was, unimaginatively, 'PetulaDeWilde.'

> Yes. Did you go to school with him?

I scrolled through some more comments; then I watched a few of the competing videos. The whole time

I kept checking my phone, hoping Jacob would call or text to apologise.

But there was nothing.

Jacob was a no-show on Monday. I told myself I didn't care.

I was at my locker just before lunch when Koula barrelled up to me. 'So? What happened? I tried texting you yesterday, like, twenty times.'

She had. I just hadn't had the energy to respond. 'They're splitting up.'

'Oh, crap. Sorry.' She gave me an awkward pat on the shoulder. I closed my locker and we started to walk down the hall. 'If it's any consolation?' she said. 'There are perks. I speak from experience. Two Christmases. Two Easter baskets. And before my mom kicked me out, my folks competed for my affection all the time. Latest iPhone, clothes, concert tickets – I got a tonne of cool stuff.'

'Um. Well. Great to know.'

We reached the cafeteria doors at the exact same moment as Rachel.

Since our craft fair outing, Rachel and I had been friendly. But we hadn't gotten together again, either.

'Petula,' she said. 'How are you?'

I couldn't help it. I burst into tears.

✳

Rachel pulled me into the closest girls' washroom. By some miracle it was deserted. 'What's wrong?'

I told her about my parents. 'And Jacob and I had a huge fight.'

'What? You didn't tell me about the fight,' said Koula. She'd followed us in, and she pushed closer to me, trying to edge Rachel out.

Rachel just manoeuvred around Koula and wrapped her arms around me.

Koula glared at her. She pried one of Rachel's arms away and wedged herself in, putting one arm around me and one around Rachel. 'Group hug!' she shouted, just as a ninth grader entered, took one look at us, and backed out the door.

Jacob texted me just before maths.

Sorry for being such a jerk. Want to explain.

Good.

Can I come over after school?

Yes.

Mom's shoes were by the door when I came home. I didn't shout out a hello, but she must have heard me anyway. A moment later she appeared in the foyer, holding Alice.

'Tula, I really wish we could talk.'

'We will. Just not now, OK? I'm tired. And Jacob's coming over.' I pulled off my sneakers. 'I forgot to tell you. I've found a forever home for Pippi.' I didn't tell her about the name change.

'Really?'

'Koula, from my art therapy class. She'll pick Pippi up on the weekend.'

'That's great news. Thank you.'

I went to my room and closed the door. I couldn't concentrate on homework, so I went online and brought up our video. Perhaps if Jacob could see some of the comments, it would give him a different perspective. Ferdinand wandered in and hopped onto my lap.

I saw that I had a reply from shirlest123.

> No I didn't go to school with Jacob.
>
> My son did.
>
> He killed my son.

THIRTY-THREE

Goose pimples sprung up on my arms.

What on earth was this person talking about?

Then I saw the link.

Shirlest123 had attached a link.

www.torontodaily/localheadlines/fatalcrash/4u384

I hovered my finger over it. Was it a joke? A virus?

I clicked.

THIRTY-FOUR

Tragedy for Northwestern Secondary

Students and staff are mourning the death of one of their classmates in a car crash on icy roads north of Toronto on Thursday. Family members confirm that Gordon Esterhasz, 17, died in the single-vehicle crash. Two other boys, including the driver of the vehicle, are still in the hospital but are expected to survive. Their names have not yet been released.

The boys were members of the Northwestern Warriors varsity basketball team and were on their way home from a tournament win when the crash occurred. 'Gord was a terrific kid, just loved life,' said Northwestern principal

Jennifer Podeswa. 'We'll be bringing in grief counsellors
to help students cope with this tragedy. Our thoughts and
prayers are with Gordon's family, and with those of the
boys who remain in the hospital.'

Police won't say whether or not alcohol was a factor
in the crash.

I didn't understand. None of it made sense. Jacob's friends
were Randle and Ben. They'd been hit by a drunk driver.

I Googled 'Gordon Esterhasz.' The first article to pop
up was an obituary.

It is with great sadness that the family of Gordon
Jonathan Esterhasz announces his sudden passing
at age 17 in a motor vehicle accident. He is survived
by his loving parents Shirley and Gordon Sr. and
siblings Ellen and Todd. Funeral services will
be held at Whitehills Chapel on March 28,
2:00 p.m. In lieu of flowers the family asks that
donations go to Mothers Against Drunk Driving.
Gordy, you will be sorely missed by countless
aunts, uncles, cousins, friends, and grandparents.

Shirley and Gordon Esterhasz. Shirley Esterhasz. S. Esterhasz.
Shirlest123.

I didn't hear the buzzer. I didn't hear my mom let him in. I only heard him when he was right behind me. 'Petula,' he began.

He stopped when he saw Gordon's obituary on my computer screen. There was a long silence.

'I was going to tell you. I came over here to tell you.'

'I don't understand.' My words were sluggish, like my mouth had been shot full of novocaine.

He stared up at the ceiling. Then he looked me in the eye.

'I was the drunk driver. I'm the one who killed Gord.'

THIRTY-FIVE

I felt dizzy. I gripped the arms of my chair. 'So, Gord Esterhasz . . .'

'Was in the car with me. Along with Frankie Goorevitch. My best friends.'

'But . . . you said their names were Randle McMurphy and Ben Willard.'

'I lied.'

My brain could not compute what he was saying. Ferdinand sat on my lap, purring loudly, oblivious.

'I've wanted to tell you so many times.'

'Tell me now.'

And so he did. Parts of his original story were true. There'd been a basketball game, near Barrie, Ontario. Gord had driven them up in his mom's station wagon.

But there were parts he'd made up. Parts he'd left out.

They were invited to a party after the game. Jacob and Frankie had just wanted to head home. But Gord wanted to go, and it was his car. So they agreed to go for an hour.

There were kegs at the party. Jacob had a few drinks. He didn't think anything of it. Gord was their designated driver.

But Gord got loaded. He could barely stand up. Frankie was pretty drunk, too.

The three of them decided that Jacob would drive.

It was snowing a lot when they left. Gord got in the backseat. Frankie sat up front. Jacob thought he was being careful. He made sure everyone was buckled up. He drove at the speed limit.

They'd been on the highway for about twenty minutes when it happened. Jacob thought they hit a patch of black ice, but he'd never know for sure. He just remembered losing control of the car. It hit the guardrail and spun. It flipped a bunch of times.

Jacob lost consciousness. When he came to, he was trapped inside the ruined car, his arm pinned under a pile of crushed metal. Frankie was beside him, unresponsive.

He couldn't see into the back. But even if he could have, he wouldn't have seen Gord. Gord had unbuckled his seat belt so he could stretch out and sleep. He'd been thrown through the windshield like a rag doll, landing thirty metres from the car.

He died on impact.

The first responders used the Jaws of Life to get Jacob and Frankie out of the car. They were taken to the hospital in the same ambulance. Jacob woke up without his arm. Frankie was paralyzed from the waist down.

Jacob was charged with impaired driving causing death. His parents hired a really good lawyer. She argued that there were extenuating circumstances, that it could have been black ice, not driver error, that caused the crash. In the end, though, the judge found Jacob guilty and sentenced him to a year in a youth facility.

As in prison, basically.

Jacob didn't tell me much about his time in juvenile detention, except to say he was on suicide watch for months.

I guess it explained why he didn't like to be in enclosed spaces.

Gord's mom started to post stuff on Jacob's Facebook page and sent him weekly letters with Bible scripture, telling him he was going to burn in hell. She thought he'd got off too easy.

He was released after six months, in November. His parents moved in December. They had been working on getting job transfers ever since the trial. They wanted to give Jacob a fresh start.

Jacob deleted all his social media accounts, which explained why I hadn't been able to find him. He told me his name never popped up in association with the accident or court case because he was a juvenile and his identity was protected.

His parents didn't leave a forwarding address and their phone numbers were unlisted. But Mrs Esterhasz found them anyway. In February the letters had started arriving again.

My brain struggled to compute everything Jacob had just told me. It was far too much to absorb. 'Why did you give your friends fake names?'

'I didn't want you to have anything to Google.'

'Is that why you said they both died?'

'I guess. I don't know.'

'But I told you the truth about Maxine. Every last detail.'

'Yes. But you don't look like a monster at the end of that story.'

The voice in my head was getting louder. *If he lied about this, what else did he lie about?*

'I was afraid you'd judge me,' he continued. 'You and the others.'

'We wouldn't have judged you.'

He shook his head. 'Not true. If I'd told you what I'd done from the start, you would have seen me in a totally different light. I wouldn't have been Jacob. I would have been Jacob, the Drunk Driver Who Killed His Friend.' He knelt down in front of me and grabbed my hands. Ferdinand leapt from my lap. 'That's where we're different. Maxine's death wasn't your fault. But with my friends . . . it *was* my fault. I've lived with the weight of this every day. And then I met you, and Ivan, and Koula, and Alonzo . . . you were all seeing the me that I was before the accident.'

'They opened up to you, too.'

'I know. And I listened. I got to know them. I got to know you. And in my own small way I tried to help. Do some good deeds. I tried to be like Clarence Odbody.'

'Who?'

'The angel who wants to earn his wings in *It's a Wonderful Life.*'

I could hear and feel my heart pounding. 'So you tried to turn your new Vancouver life into the plot of a movie.'

'No. I don't know.'

'And the rest of us were supporting characters.'

'No! Of course not. Look, nothing I do will take away what happened. But at least when I was focused on helping you and the others I could feel OK about myself for brief moments of time.'

A truly awful thought struck me. 'Does this mean *I* was a good deed?'

What he did next broke my heart.

He hesitated.

'Oh my God.' The room tilted sideways. I hadn't had a fainting spell in months and I really didn't want to have one now.

'Listen to me, Petula. Yes, at first, I thought I could help you get over some of your irrational fears. Help you loosen up a bit—'

'Loosen up?' A wave of nausea crashed over me. Suddenly everything made so much sense.

'But then I started falling for you, and all your quirks. I fell for you big-time—'

'Why should I believe you? *How* can I believe you?'

'Because it's me. You can trust me.'

I lost it. 'Listen to yourself! You lied to me, Jacob, you lied to all of us. I mean, Jesus – you killed someone! And we had *no idea*. Because you're a *really good liar.*' Another awful thought struck me. 'Were you lying when you said you loved me?'

'I can't believe you're asking me that.'

'Really? You can't? How can I trust a word that comes out of your mouth? How do I know you like the shark socks I made you? How do I know your middle name is Schlomo?' I felt the bile surge into my throat. I wasn't going to faint. But I was going to be sick. I grabbed my garbage can just in time.

Jacob placed his hand on my back while I retched.

'Don't touch me. Please, just go. I need you to leave.'

'Petula, please—'

'Go!'

When I finally lifted my head, he was gone.

THIRTY-SIX

I didn't go to school the next day.

I got out of bed and went through the motions of getting ready, but once my parents left for work I crawled back under the covers. It felt like I'd been plunged into a vat of molasses. My movements were slow and sluggish. I watched a lot of daytime TV surrounded by cats.

The school left an automated message informing my parents that I'd been absent, but I deleted it before either of them got home.

Rachel texted. *U ok?*

Koula texted, too. *Bitch, what up?*

Bad flu, I typed.

Not a peep from Jacob.

But I heard from Shirley Esterhasz. She'd found me on Facebook and sent me a private message.

> So Jacob Cohen's making cat videos. How nice for him that his life is moving on, while my son's life is over. Is this who you want for your friend? Think about it.

Part of me couldn't blame her. I knew grief could make you do crazy things. Mean things.

But still. I deleted her message. I changed my privacy settings. And I blocked Shirley Esterhasz.

I also Googled Randle McMurphy and Ben Willard. Jack Nicholson played Randle McMurphy in *One Flew Over the Cuckoo's Nest*. Martin Sheen played Captain Ben Willard in *Apocalypse Now*.

Of course.

For the first time in months I searched for articles for my scrapbook and printed them.

Mexican Man Suffers Death by Cow

Forty-five-year-old Carlos Rodriguez was killed when a cow fell through his roof and landed on him. The cow had been lifted from a neighbouring field when a tornado ripped through the region on Saturday night . . .

Woman Watering Plants
Plummets to Her Death

Sixty-six-year-old Bessie Higgins kept beautiful window boxes at her seventh-storey apartment in Manhattan. 'Everyone in the neighbourhood loved looking at them,' said a woman who lived across the street. But on Sunday, Bessie leaned out a little too far to do some pruning, and . . .

The whole time, my mind kept running in circles with the same questions

Why had I ever let my guard down?

Why had I been so gullible?

Why had I let myself believe that Jacob was genuinely interested in me?

Why had I believed he was an authentic human being?

Optimism had snuck up behind me and bitten me right in the ass.

THIRTY-SEVEN

On Wednesday I stayed home again. I was getting oddly entranced by the world of daytime TV. There was *The Talk*, which was not to be confused with *The View*; there was *Let's Make a Deal* and *The Price Is Right*; there was high drama for shiny, blandly attractive people who were either *The Young and the Restless* or *The Bold and the Beautiful*. Watching the shows stilled the chatter in my brain.

When the school left another automated message, I deleted that, too.

I knew Mom would be home around four, so at three-thirty I forced myself to get out of my penguin onesie and put on normal clothes.

She made us scrambled eggs and toast for supper. The

two of us ate in front of the TV. Alice, Stanley, and Stuart Little chased each other around the room while Moominmamma watched, looking disdainful. Ferdinand and Pippi were curled up on Mom's lap, and Anne of Green Gables was curled up on mine.

'Can we talk about the separation?' Mom asked during a commercial break.

'What's there to talk about?'

'I don't know. How you're feeling . . . if there's anything we can do to make the transition easier . . .' Ferdinand rolled onto his back and stretched, pushing Pippi out of the way. Mom rubbed his belly.

'There is something.'

'Name it.'

'I want you to stop bringing home more cats. Volunteer for Feline Rescue, yes. But don't bring any more felines home.'

Mom looked startled. 'I didn't expect this from you. Your dad, yes. But not you.'

'That's because I've spent the last two years trying to please you both. But I don't have to do that any more.'

'No. You don't.'

'I love the cats, you know I do. But this – this is too much. It's too much money. It's too much work. I spend a lot of time cleaning up after them. I don't think you notice how much. It's not fair to the cats and it's not fair to me.'

She was quiet for a moment. I was worried she might start to cry, but she didn't. 'OK. Point taken.'

We got up and took the dishes into the kitchen. I was scrubbing the frying pan when she said, 'Tula, are things OK between you and Jacob?'

I wondered if she'd heard us arguing. I just shook my head.

'Do you want to talk about it?'

'No. I really don't.'

She looked worried, but she didn't push me.

I had so many conflicting feelings, I didn't know what to do with them. I felt terribly sorry for Jacob one moment, then furious and betrayed the next.

And I missed him. Or at least I missed the Jacob I thought I knew.

His silence confirmed my worst fear:

I'd been just another good deed.

And also.

He'd killed a friend. Put another in a wheelchair.

It was hard for me to wrap my brain around all of that.

Lies or no lies, I didn't know if I could ever look at him the same way again.

He'd been right.

I did judge.

THIRTY-EIGHT

When I didn't go to school again on Thursday, Mr Watley called and left a message. 'Hello, this is the principal at Princess Margaret Secondary, Ronald Watley.' Ronald. How had I never known his first name? 'I'm concerned that Petula hasn't been at school for three days in a row. Please call me back at your earliest convenience.'

I deleted the message and put a reminder in my phone to call the school back at five p.m., when the office would be closed. Then I left my own message. 'Hello, Ronald, this is Virginia De Wilde. Petula's been home sick with the flu this week. My apologies for not calling earlier.'

Rachel's texts got more persistent throughout the day.

She called a few times. Koula's texts got angrier. They started with *Where u?* and ended with *Bitch, answer me!!*

At three-thirty, someone buzzed the apartment. I was curled up on the couch, surrounded by cats, in the midst of another marathon session of daytime TV. A large woman was throwing a chair at another large woman on a talk show. The theme was 'Is Your Husband a Serial Cheater?'

It was far too riveting for me to bother getting up.

On Friday morning at eight, the buzzer sounded again. I was still in bed, but my parents were up and about, so I couldn't stop them from letting the person in.

What if it's Jacob? I thought. I buried myself under the covers.

'She's in her room,' I heard my dad say from the hall.

A moment later my door opened. 'I am not letting you shut yourself off from me again, Petula. You need to tell me what's going on.'

Rachel.

I told her everything.

When I was finished, she said, 'Poor Jacob.'

'Really? That's the best you've got?'

'I'm just saying. Imagine what it must be like for him, living with what he's done.'

'I guess.'

'He hasn't been at school, either.'

'I kind of figured.'

She squeezed my hand. 'I'm really sorry, Petula. What a lousy week you've had.'

'My mind just won't shut up. Now I think everything he told me was a lie. *Everything.*'

She got my meaning. 'I don't believe that. I've seen the way he looks at you. He's crazy about you. He couldn't fake that.'

There was a knock on the door. 'Get a move on, girls,' Dad said. 'Or you'll be late for school.'

'He's right,' Rachel said.

'I'm not going.'

Rachel turned around and dug into her bag. When she turned back, she was wearing her *Little House on the Prairie* bonnet. 'You know something, Mary?' she said in her best Laura Ingalls voice.

'No . . . what?' I answered as Mary.

'Life sure is a lot easier when you don't like boys!'

That made me laugh, just a little.

Rachel stood up and held out her hands. 'Let's go.'

'I can't.'

'Yes, you can. I'm not leaving till you do.' She grabbed my wrists and pulled me upright. Her nose wrinkled in disgust. 'Gross. You reek.' With the bonnet still on her head, she switched to her Nellie Oleson voice. 'Half the time, you don't even smell like a girl, Laura Ingalls! You're either sweaty, or you stink of fish!'

'Well, I sweat a lot and I fish a lot!' I answered, or rather Laura Ingalls did.

'Seriously,' Rachel said in her own voice. 'Shower. Now.'

I looked at her in her bonnet.

I wasn't going to blow it this time, so I did as I was told.

One good thing about being unpopular is that no one seemed to notice I hadn't been at school all week.

Except for Mr Watley. He spotted me as I was heading to YART. 'Petula. You need to come see me after school.'

'OK, Ronald,' I said without thinking.

His eyebrows shot up.

When I walked into YART, Koula, Alonzo, and Ivan were already at the table. Koula leapt up and barrelled towards me. At first I thought she was coming in for another awkward hug. But no. She slugged me really hard on the arm. 'Ow!'

'That's for not answering my texts. Then she slugged me again. 'I was worried!'

'I'm sorry,' I said. Tears sprang to my eyes. 'It's been a truly lousy time. First my parents. And Jacob—'

'I know.'

'No, you don't.'

'Yes, I do.'

'No, you don't.'

'Yes, I do.'

'No, you—'

'Would you two cut it out,' Alonzo said. 'We do. Jacob sent all of us a long email. He told us everything.'

Oh.

Betty stepped out of her office. She wore a bright blue suit with yellow buttons down the front.

'Holy crap, you're like a living, breathing ad for Ikea,' blurted Koula. Without being told, she dug into her pocket and tossed a quarter onto the table. Betty put it in the almost-full mason jar.

'Jacob contacted me, too,' Betty told us. 'We had a long phone chat earlier today.' She hooked up her laptop to the TV monitor. 'He also sent me Koula's finished video. I thought we could watch it.'

Jacob had edited the video to 'All Apologies,' by Nirvana. Koula's signs and facial expressions had us laughing one moment, tearing up the next.

When it was over, Betty turned up the lights. Koula

grabbed a Kleenex and blew her nose. 'That was really freaking good.'

'No matter what, he's a great storyteller,' said Alonzo.

'And a great liar,' I said.

'Let's talk about that,' said Betty. 'Who would like to go first? Ivan? How are you feeling?'

Ivan had been silent until now. 'Mad.' He rocked back and forth in his chair, a scowl on his face.

'Why mad?'

'Because he lied. Because he did something dumb.' I had the unkind thought that Ivan would never grow up to be a speechwriter.

'Alonzo?'

Alonzo looked at his fingernails, which were painted dark red. 'I'm ... I can't compute what I know now, with the guy I thought I knew. One minute I feel really angry with him. I mean, drunk driving, who does that any more? The next minute I feel awful for him. For what it must be like to live with this. And then ... then I think about his victims. The boy who died. What that must be like for the family.'

Koula nodded. 'I felt super angry when I first read his email. Like I'd just been sucker punched. For twenty-four hours I wanted to kill him. I couldn't figure out why I was *so* angry, like, *rage* angry. So, um ...' She mumbled the next part.

I leaned forward. 'Pardon?'

'I came to see Betty,' she said.

Betty smiled. 'We had a good talk, didn't we?'

'Yeah, we did.' Koula looked at the rest of us. 'You'd be surprised. She's pretty good one-on-one. Not the total idiot you'd expect.'

Betty coughed. 'Do you want to share what you told me?'

Koula tugged at her fishnets. 'Once, when I was high, I stole my dad's car. I hit a mailbox and broke one of the headlights.

'But that mailbox could have been a kid, you know? I was mad at Jacob, sure, but I was also mad at myself. It so easily could have been me in his shoes. I didn't set out to hurt anyone, but I was just lucky I didn't. He wasn't so lucky. But he also wasn't malicious. He didn't mean to hurt anyone, either.'

'But he did,' Ivan said.

'Yes. He did,' said Alonzo. 'It was an idiotic thing to do.'

'Remember when we talked about guilt that one night?' asked Koula. 'Imagine his guilt.'

'Petula?' said Betty. 'Is there anything you'd like to add?'

I tried to gather my thoughts. 'I feel for him, too. But he lied to us. Repeatedly. We told him everything. He told us only what he wanted us to hear.'

'Have any of you spoken to Jacob since he shared his story?'

We all shook our heads.

Betty looked at each of us. 'He must be feeling very isolated.' I couldn't tell whether or not she was giving us a slap on the wrist.

We all fell silent. Eventually Alonzo spoke. 'I'm leaning towards forgiveness. I mean, there are a lot of people who will never be able to forgive him. And he'll never be able to forgive himself. Maybe we don't need to punish him too.'

Koula leaned back in her chair and crossed her arms over her chest. 'I'm with Alonzo.'

I shook my head. 'Really? It's that simple? After everything he did to us?'

'What, exactly, did he do to *us*?' said Alonzo. 'Bring us closer together? Make us feel happy and proud and creative once in a while?'

'What a monster,' added Koula.

I did not appreciate the sarcasm.

'Plus there's everything he did for you,' said Koula, looking at me.

'What did he do for me except lie and lead me on?'

Koula guffawed. 'Seriously? You need me to spell it out? You were this paranoid little freak. Constantly dousing yourself in hand sanitiser. Leading this narrow, sad little life.'

'Scared of everything,' Alonzo added.

Ivan nodded. 'You were weird, Petula.' This from the boy who sometimes answered questions with farts.

'Jacob resuscitated you,' said Koula.

'It's true,' said Alonzo. 'We're all witnesses. He brought you back to life.'

I couldn't believe it. I felt completely ganged up on. I looked at Betty, to see if she was going to do something, chastise them, maybe, or make them put a quarter in the Jar.

She was *nodding in agreement*. Highly unprofessional.

Easy for all of you to talk about forgiveness, I wanted to shout. *You didn't have sex with him. You didn't have sex with a boy who forgot to tell you he'd killed someone, and who treated you as a pity project.*

You didn't tell him you loved him, over and over again.

Fifteen minutes later I sat across from Mr Watley in the chair with the nubby multicoloured fabric. The grooves didn't mould quite so perfectly to my bum any more.

I tried to focus. I was still reeling from the pile-on at YART.

Mr Watley steepled his hands under his chin. 'So. The flu.'

'That's right.' I coughed a few times for effect.

'The voicemail your mother left yesterday. It sounded a lot like you.'

'People confuse the two of us on the phone all the time.'

He stared at me with his watery eyes. 'Mr Cohen hasn't been here all week, either.'

'I don't know anything about that.' I sat back in the nubby chair. It was rather nice being back in Mr Watley's office. Comforting and familiar, like a pair of old slippers.

But I did notice one change. A pottery bowl with a lid had taken the place of my mason jar snow globe on his desk. I felt a tug of envy that someone else's craft had usurped mine.

Mr Watley picked up a thick folder. 'I'd like you to take him his homework.'

'What? Why me?'

'Because you're friends.'

'Not any more.'

'Petula, I'm not asking you to marry him and raise a family.' He pushed the folder across the desk. 'Just take him his damn homework.'

I didn't pick the folder up. 'Who gave you the pottery, sir?'

'It's an urn. It holds Martha's ashes.'

My heart sank. 'Your wife?'

'Goodness, no! Our pug. She lived a good, long life. But still . . . her absence is keenly felt.'

'I'm really sorry.'

'Thank you. Now will you please take Mr Cohen's homework and go? I have a golf game in half an hour and I don't want to miss my tee time.'

I looked at the folder. I looked at the urn. 'Tell you what.'

'What?'

'I'll bring Jacob his homework if you do something for me in return.'

He sighed. 'Petula, are you trying to bribe me?'

I thought for a moment. 'I suppose that's one way of looking at it, yes.'

THIRTY-NINE

Mr Watley had reluctantly agreed to my deal, so I kept my end of the bargain. I walked to Jacob's apartment and left his homework with Serge the Concierge.

Probably not what Mr Watley had in mind, but too bad.

The next morning, Saturday, I texted Rachel and asked if she wanted to come over.

She texted back *yes*.

My parents were over the moon to see Rachel at our place two days in a row after almost two years. They fussed over her in an embarrassing way. When we finally escaped to my bedroom, she dumped out the contents of her tote bag on my floor. 'It's everything we need to make those cheese-grater earring holders.'

I was fixing little metallic feet to the base of a grater with my glue gun when she asked, 'Have you heard from Jacob?'

'No.'

'Have you reached out to him?'

'Can we not talk about it? I don't mean to be rude. It's just— I don't want to think about him, or any of it. Just for a little while.'

'Of course.' And for the next hour we crafted together, chatting about nothing in particular. It was wonderful.

At eleven the buzzer sounded, announcing the arrival of the Watleys. 'This should be interesting,' Rachel said. 'I've never seen Mr Watley out of his natural habitat before.'

Mom let them in. 'Hello,' said Mr Watley. 'I'm Ronald, and this is my wife, Ethel.'

Rachel and I did our best not to stare, but it was anthropologically fascinating, seeing Mr Watley outside of school. He wore loose-fitting old-people jeans, a golf shirt, and bright orange socks. Mrs Watley – Ethel – was equally intriguing. She was all about multiple floral prints. I immediately admired her and her bold fashion choices.

'Can we offer you some tea?' asked Mom.

'That sounds lovely,' said Ethel.

We settled into the living room. I found Alice and

Stanley, and put Alice on Mr Watley's lap and Stanley on Ethel's.

'What sweet things!' Mrs Watley said. 'They're like two peas in a pod.'

'Do you think it would be all right if we changed their names to Fred and Ginger?' asked Mr Watley.

I thought about Koula, who'd picked up Pippi-slash-Lorena Bobbitt with her dad the night before. 'Fred and Ginger are great names,' I said.

The Watleys had brought along their pug's carrier, so when it was time for them to leave, they took Alice and Stanley with them. I gave them a bunch of catnip toys I'd made. Mom kept it together surprisingly well. 'I'm happy they're going to a loving home,' she said.

After the Watleys had left, Rachel and I finished our earring holders. At around five o'clock she got a text from her mom. 'My parents are wondering if you'd like to come for dinner,' she said.

She watched me closely. I took longer to answer than was polite.

This was it. It was now or never.

'OK.'

Rachel lived on the main floor of an old heritage home in the heart of the West End. Her parents had bought it years ago and renovated it, and now rented out the basement and top floor.

We walked up the front steps together. I felt sick with trepidation. Rachel unlocked the door and stepped inside.

I stayed where I was.

Rachel's parents, Holger and Hilda, appeared in the foyer. 'Petula. It's so good to see you again.' Holger, a big bear of a man, pulled me inside. Both he and Hilda gave me a hug.

'I'm making macaroni with three cheeses for dinner,' Holger said.

I smiled. He knew it was my favourite dish, along with his grilled three-cheese sandwiches and quattro formaggi pizzas. Rachel's family loves cheese. 'That sounds amazing,' I said.

'I was sorry to hear about your parents' separation,' Hilda said. 'Rachel told me.' She squeezed my arm.

'You girls can go on into the living room. We'll holler when food's ready,' said Holger.

'See? That wasn't so hard, was it?' asked Rachel.

I shook my head. 'No. It wasn't.'

We headed into the living room.

Owen was sitting on the couch, watching a *Blue's Clues* rerun.

He was so cute. He still had apple-red cheeks and a

shock of blond hair, but he was a little bit leaner, a little bit taller.

'Hey, Owen,' said Rachel. 'Remember Petula?'

Owen looked at me. I held my breath. Last time I'd seen him, he'd screamed that I'd killed his sister.

'Steve doesn't need strawberries for the banana cake,' he said to me.

'Are you sure?' I asked.

'Yes.'

'I'm going to go help my parents,' said Rachel. She left the room. It was a stinker of a move.

I stood where I was.

'He needs two cups of flour,' Owen said, still looking at me.

'I think maybe it's three cups,' I said.

'No, silly! It's two.' He bounced up and down on the couch. 'Come sit.'

I perched beside him on the couch. He watched the TV, and I watched him.

Yes, he made me think of Maxine. But seeing him didn't make me feel worse. It didn't make me miss her any more or any less.

Owen didn't make me miss Maxine because he wasn't Maxine.

'A clue!' he shouted.

'Where?' I said, pretending I couldn't see it.

'There!' He pointed at the screen.

'Where?'

'There, silly.'

This is what I was so afraid of. This little boy. The thought made me laugh. Which made Owen laugh.

We watched *Blue's Clues* and giggled until Holger called us in to supper.

FORTY

On Sunday, a guy came by the apartment to pick up hundreds of Dad's records. Dad had advertised a large chunk of his collection on an audiophile website. 'I can't move them all to the new place,' he said. 'I don't have room.' He let me keep my favourites, and he kept all of his favourites, too.

The buyer was rake-thin, in his fifties. 'I'm Cecil,' he said. He wore a purple tie-dyed shirt and his long hair was pulled back with a scrunchie.

Dad and I helped him load the boxes of records into his Toyota Corolla. When we'd loaded the last box, Cecil handed Dad a cheque. 'Did I spell the name right?'

'You did. Thank you.'

'No, thank *you*,' said Cecil. 'This is a wonderful addition to my collection.' He drove away.

Dad handed the cheque to me. 'This is for you.' I looked at it. It was made out to Petula De Wilde.

And it was for over three thousand dollars.

That's right: over three *thousand* dollars.

There were a million ways my parents could use this money. 'Dad, I can't—'

He cut me off. 'We'll put most of it in your education fund and deposit the rest in your bank account for a rainy day.'

I didn't know what to say. Was it guilt money?

Who was I to say no to guilt money?

So I just said, 'Thanks.'

FORTY-ONE

On Tuesday I stopped by Mr Watley's office to pick up Jacob's homework again. That was part of our arrangement: I would do twice-weekly deliveries until Jacob came back to school. 'How are Fred and Ginger settling in?'

'Extremely well. Ethel is smitten, and truth be told, so am I.' Mr Watley handed me a folder. 'I don't mean to pry, but how is Mr Cohen?'

'I wouldn't know.'

'But you saw him just last week.'

I shook my head. 'I left his homework with the concierge.'

He looked at me with his watery eyes. 'Petula . . .'

'What? Why can't everyone get off my back? I'm doing

what you asked. If you're so curious, *you* go visit him.' I strode out of the office, stuffing the folder into my tote bag.

Why were people acting like *I* was the disappointment?

I walked to Jacob's apartment, taking deep breaths as I passed the construction site. I still felt angry. When I was a block away, a man called out behind me. 'Petula.'

I turned, keys between my knuckles.

It was Jacob's dad, David. He had dark circles under his eyes, like he hadn't slept in a while. 'Do you have a moment?' he asked. 'Can we walk around the block?'

No! my mind shouted. *No, I don't have a moment; no, I don't want to walk around the block with you.* 'Um. OK,' I said. 'You're home early.'

'We don't think Jacob should be alone right now. Miranda and I are taking turns.'

Oh.

We started walking. 'I know he told you,' David said. I nodded.

'He's been wanting to tell you for quite a while. I was the one who told him he shouldn't.' He was hunched over, like a little old man. 'He's a beautiful soul, Petula. I know I'm his dad, but it's not just me. If you could have known him in Toronto . . . he was the kid all the other kids liked. He was the kid who intervened when there were conflicts. He could move so easily between different cliques . . . He made people feel like they could be their best selves. Miranda and I would joke all the time, how did we luck out? How did we get a kid who is so much better than the best of the two of us?' His voice cracked, and he turned away for a moment. 'And then all of this happened. Our beautiful boy made a terrible mistake. And watching him suffer, watching the other families suffer . . . I'm his dad, I should be able to do something.' David started to cry. I had no idea what to do, so I looked away.

'When he met you, and the others, it was the first time we saw a spark of his old self. You've made a huge difference to him. I want you to know that.'

'OK.' That was my contribution to the most awkward conversation of my life.

We'd looped back and stood outside their building. I rummaged in my tote bag and pulled out the folder. 'Jacob's homework.'

David took the folder from me. I thought I was free and clear, but then he opened the door and held it for me. 'You're coming up, right?' His look was pleading.

I didn't know what to do. I stepped inside. Serge the Concierge said hello. David pressed the elevator button.

I saw my cowardly out. 'I don't do elevators,' I said. 'But you go ahead. I'll take the stairs.' When he got on the elevator, I would turn around and leave.

'I'll take the stairs with you,' he said. 'I could use the exercise.'

I had no more tricks up my sleeve.

Miranda was on the couch working on her laptop when we entered. 'Oh! Petula.' She got up and embraced me. She looked exhausted. 'It's good to see you.'

'She's come to see Jacob,' said David.

No, I haven't!

'He'll be happy to see you,' said Miranda.

She led me down the hall and knocked quietly on his bedroom door. My heart was pounding in my chest.

'Jacob,' she said, opening the door a crack. 'Petula is here.'

Jacob was a lump under the covers. His robotic arm rested on the bedside table. The room smelled funky, like he hadn't left it for a long time.

Jacob rolled over and opened his eyes. When he saw me, he smiled. 'Hey.'

'I'll leave you two,' said Miranda.

Part of me wanted to fling myself on the bed and hold him. Part of me wanted to fling myself on the bed and pummel him.

I stayed by the door.

'I'm sorry,' he said. 'I should have been honest from the start.'

'Yeah. You should have.'

We both fell silent.

'When I met you,' he began, 'you were so . . . odd.'

Not off to a great start.

'But so beautiful.'

Better.

'And, I don't know. Broken. Like me. And when we started hanging out . . . for the first time I didn't feel like a total piece of garbage twenty-four seven.'

I knew all about feeling like garbage.

'I love you, Petula. That was never a lie.'

I wanted to believe him. I took a few steps towards his bed. 'Koula and Alonzo want you to come back to YART.'

'What about Ivan?'

'He's angry.'

'What about you?'

'Yes.'

Tears started rolling down his face. 'This is going to be my life. I'll meet people, we'll get along. At some point I'll have to tell them what I did. And then I'll watch them pull away.'

'You don't know that.'

'Based on the evidence so far, I can guess.'

I sat down on his bed.

'Do I stink?'

I leaned in close and sniffed. 'Yes.'

'How about my breath?' He breathed on me.

'Gross.'

He took my hand.

'I have to ask you something,' I said. 'Why haven't you reached out to Frankie?'

'Because . . . he's better off never hearing from me again.'

'And maybe because you're scared?'

'That, too.' We fell into silence. 'I have to ask you something, too,' he said after a while. 'And you have to tell the truth.'

'OK.'

'Will you be able to forgive me for everything I did? Will you be able to look at me the same way?'

I opened my mouth.

And I couldn't do it. I couldn't break his heart.

So for the first time I told Jacob a lie.

I said, 'Yes.'

FORTY-TWO

The fog in my head started to clear.

I kept bringing Jacob his homework, upping it to three days a week. Alonzo and Koula often came with me. The first time Koula saw Jacob she punched him in the arm, but he just grabbed her with his real hand and rubbed her Mohawk with his bionic one.

I was nice when I saw him.

But I still kept my distance.

Jacob returned to school in May. Things went OK. Word hadn't spread. I thought that was a small miracle, and said so on his first time back at YART.

'Why's that surprising?' asked Koula. 'We're practically the only ones who know.'

'Yes, but you in particular are not known for your discretion.'

'Shut your piehole,' she said. Betty indicated the Jar. Koula dropped in a quarter, then she placed something else on the table. 'It's my two-month chip.'

'Wow,' said Alonzo. 'That's twice as long as you've ever made it before.'

'I detect a hint of sarcasm in your tone, and I am choosing to ignore it.'

Alonzo wrapped her in a hug. 'No sarcasm. Seriously. You should be proud.'

'Yes, you should,' said Betty. 'Congratulations.'

Koula turned to Jacob. 'And also, I sent my mom the video we made. I didn't hear anything at first, but two days ago she phoned me. We met at a coffee shop yesterday after school. Neutral territory. And we only shouted a little bit. Mostly we just talked.'

'I'm happy to hear that,' said Jacob.

'Yeah. That's fantastic,' said Alonzo. But he sounded a bit glum. He hadn't heard a word from his family. Not a peep.

Jacob turned to Ivan, who'd been sullen and quiet so far. 'How've you been doing?'

Ivan wouldn't look him in the eye. He just shrugged.

'I've really missed you,' Jacob said.

Ivan didn't answer.

'I have tickets to a Whitecaps game next weekend. I was hoping we could go together.'

Ivan couldn't help himself. 'Good seats?'

'Great seats.'

Ivan cracked a smile.

Betty cleared her throat. 'I also have some good news. I passed my course. I'll be moving on to a temporary position with elementary-age children next September.'

We congratulated her. After Betty went into her office, Koula emptied the mason jar that she'd almost single-handedly filled with quarters.

The following Friday we brought in a cake, party hats, and noisemakers to celebrate.

We even put socks on our hands. Our puppets belted out 'For She's a Jolly Good Fellow.'

Dad's impending move had put the three of us into a spring-cleaning frenzy. The weekend before he was scheduled to leave, I did a massive clean-up of my room. I filled one bag with garbage and another bag with old scarves, hats, socks, and mittens I'd knitted over the years. They would go to a homeless shelter in our neighbourhood. I cleared out the clutter from under my bed. Including my scrapbook.

I flipped through it.

I put it in the garbage bag.

I took it out of the garbage bag.

I left it beside the garbage bag.

Lastly, I went through my books. I packed up a couple of boxes to donate to a school and reorganised the rest.

That's how I found, tucked at the back of one of the shelves, Maxine's copy of *Where the Wild Things Are*.

It was a worn, much-loved hardcover. I opened it up. *To Maxine Ella, our own little wild thing: may your life be full of adventure and joy. With love from Mommy and Daddy and big sister Petula.*

I sat on my bedroom floor and had a good cry.

Then I put the book back on the shelf. Not hidden in the back. But not too prominent, either.

Just there, always.

FORTY-THREE

On Saturday morning, Dad's moving day, he made us one
last pancake breakfast before picking up the rental van.
We were just finishing breakfast when our buzzer sounded.
I leapt up to answer it.

'Delivery for Petula De Wilde,' said a woman's voice.

I buzzed her up. Mom had wandered into the foyer.
'Do you know what it is?'

'No idea.'

All three of us were curious. I opened the door and we
glanced towards the elevators.

A moment later a woman in a Canada Post uniform
stepped off wheeling a dolly that held the biggest bag of
dry cat food I'd ever seen in my life and six large packs
of canned food.

I signed for the delivery. A card was attached. *Congratulations on winning one of ten runner-up prizes in our Purrfect video contest!*

I don't know why, exactly, but I laughed for a long time.

An hour later I was carrying a heavy box out to Dad's rental van when I saw him, standing on the pavement. We hadn't seen each other outside his apartment or school for quite a while. It was a cool morning, and he was wearing his off-white fisherman's sweater.

My favourite.

'Need an extra set of hands?' he asked. 'One real, one artificial?'

'Sure.'

He opened the back of the van for me. I told him about the runner-up prize. 'No way,' Jacob said. 'That's pretty cool.'

'Not exactly an Academy Award, but still.'

'Maybe we could shoot another *Cataptation* sometime.'

I looked at him, surprised. 'Yeah. Maybe.'

We headed inside to get another load of stuff, and ran into my parents in the foyer. They knew Jacob's story by now; I'd told them an abbreviated version. They both gave him a big hug. 'I can't tell you how happy we are to see you again,' Mom said.

When we'd finished loading Dad's things, Jacob helped me carry down the boxes and bags from my room. We put the books and knit goods into the van so Dad and I could drop them off on our way to his new apartment.

Then we carried the garbage bag and my scrapbook to the back of the building.

Jacob hurled the garbage bag upward and got it in a dumpster.

I stared at my scrapbook for a long time. I got ready to throw it.

Something held me back.

'Petula.'

I threw it. But my aim was crappy; it bounced off the side of the bin and landed at my feet.

'Maybe it's a sign,' I began.

Jacob picked it up and chucked it into the dumpster. 'There. Done.'

Corny as it sounds, I felt a little bit lighter. I turned towards him. 'I've really missed you.' There. I'd said it.

'I've really missed you, too.' He took my hands. 'If I try to hug you, do you promise not to knee me in the nuts?'

'Promise.'

He hugged me.

I hugged him back.

After a while, I pressed myself against him.

He pressed back.

My face was squished against his sweater. The mothball smell was still there, coupled with his deodorant and his soap, and also the smell that was just him.

When he started kissing me, I kissed him back.

'Can we try again?' he asked.

'I don't know.'

But we kept kissing until my dad hollered for me. His voice startled both of us, and pressed together as we were, we lost our balance.

But we held on. We didn't fall.

EPILOGUE

I keep forgetting to breathe.

When I remember, I suck in air, inhaling and exhaling like I've just run a marathon. I grab the safety instructions from the pouch in front of me and try to focus on the drawings.

Jacob puts his real hand over mine. 'You're going to be fine. This is one of the safest modes of transportation ever.'

Suddenly the plane shudders forward. 'Oh my God, we're moving.'

'We're still on the ground. We're just taxiing.'

I'm wearing my lucky everything: lucky earrings, lucky Rachel-made necklace, lucky hand-woven belt. I touch them all, my own weird version of making the sign of the cross.

The flight attendants start to run through the safety features on the plane.

Jacob pulls out a Twix bar. 'You want some—'

'Shh!' I say. I need to hear everything. I want to know how, exactly, they expect us to jump out of an emergency exit and propel ourselves down an inflatable slide while blowing up an inflatable life jacket. It sounds like something to take our minds off the fact that we are facing sure death.

I'm in the middle seat. Jacob is by the window. The woman in the aisle seat keeps shooting me sideways glances.

When the flight attendants are done I speak loudly to the one closest to us. 'Excuse me, sir, I just have a few more questions—'

'No. You don't.' Jacob smiles sweetly at the flight attendant. 'She doesn't.' He settles back in his seat, adjusting the monkey neck pillow I made him especially for the trip.

'Flight attendants, prepare for departure,' says the captain over the PA.

As the plane heads down the runway, picking up speed, I squeeze my eyes shut. Jacob grips my hand.

Suddenly everything feels different. Smoother. Lighter. 'We're airborne,' says Jacob.

I dare to open my eyes. I peek out the window. Sure enough, we're above Vancouver. I can see all of Stanley Park, and the North Shore Mountains. It is beautiful and terrifying at the same time.

But over the next few hours, as some of my fear seeps away, I see it creep into Jacob. He grows quiet as we fly over the Rockies, then the prairies.

He's not afraid of the journey.

He's afraid of the arrival.

I got the idea for this trip during a session with my new counsellor.

Mr Watley told me about him in his office one day. He had a new framed photo on his desk; this one showed him holding up Alice/Ginger and Mrs Watley holding up Stanley/Fred.

'He's a brand-new hire. I've met him and I like him. I thought you might like to try him out.'

I was wary at first. My one-on-one sessions with Carol had been disastrous. But after just two visits, I realised the new counsellor and I were going to get along just fine. He's the real deal. For one thing, I'm pretty sure he's been through some hard times too. Call it a sixth sense.

His name is Cosmo Economopoulos, and I can talk to him about everything. Plus he's already asked me to make a pair of Scrabble tile earrings for his wife, because she's apparently a total Scrabble nerd.

We talk a lot about Maxine. We discuss my parents, who, I have to admit, seem to be doing better now that they're living apart. We discuss my new living arrangement, half the week at Mom's, half the week at Dad's.

It isn't so bad. Mom and I talk a lot. And Dad doesn't work late on the days I'm with him. His place is small but charming, in an old, regal-looking redbrick low-rise called Robson Arms. My bedroom has an actual window seat overlooking the treetops – a perfect reading perch.

Sometimes Dad puts on music. He kept over two hundred records, so there's always something to listen to. Sometimes we even dance like we used to. And Rachel and I have been having a crafting heyday, decorating my new bedroom and adding lots of cool touches around Dad's apartment, like hand-stitched throw cushions, macramé wall hangings, and even some old-school doilies.

I'm not sure Dad likes everything we've done so far. But he doesn't dare say a word.

Guilt has its upside.

There's one subject Cosmo and I circle back to over and over, and that's Jacob.

I still struggle to trust him. Sometimes, when he's telling me a story, I wonder if it's really true.

And I still find it hard to look at him the same way as before.

Cosmo says all of this is normal. He says I can only take it day by day and see how it plays out. 'It sounds like he's a good person at heart.'

'Yes.'

'A good person who did a bad thing.'

'Yes.'

'From everything you've told me, he's been a positive presence in your life.'

'He has. No question. He's helped me face a lot of my fears.'

'Have you ever thought that you might be able to help him face his?'

I took what Cosmo said to heart. I thought about it a lot. And I came up with an idea. I told Cosmo about it at our next session. 'It's interesting,' he said. 'But you'll have to get Jacob and his family on board.'

I didn't go about it quite that way. Instead I used the rainy-day money in my bank account and bought two non-refundable tickets to Toronto during a seat sale.

Then I told Jacob my plan.

He said no.

'Fine. But I'm getting on that plane, no matter what.'

'You. Getting on a plane. Alone.'

'Yes.' It was the second lie I'd told him. No way would I get on that plane without him.

At the last minute, he agreed to come. He talked it over with his parents first. They had mixed feelings but felt that it was Jacob's decision to make.

My parents didn't love the idea, but when they found out we'd be staying with Jacob's bubbe and zadie, they relaxed.

Koula, Alonzo, and Ivan took the Canada Line to the airport with Jacob and me to see us off. Ivan wore the Whitecaps hat Jacob had bought him. Koula slugged Jacob on the arm, then gave me a big hug. Alonzo followed us as we got in the security line. Then he pretended to hit an invisible wall. He took a few steps back and ran to join us. He hit the wall again.

Miming at its best.

When we boarded the plane, we had to show photo ID. I snuck a peek at Jacob's.

His middle name really is Schlomo.

We're beginning our descent into Toronto. I've done remarkably well. I only spent fifty per cent of my time wondering if any of the other passengers were planning to hijack the plane or detonate a bomb.

We'll be in Toronto for a week. Jacob's going to take me to his favourite vintage clothing store and the Art Gallery of Ontario and the Royal Ontario Museum. He also wants me to go up the CN Tower even though I've told him 'over my dead body.'

And we're going to visit Frankie.

Jacob sent him a message. Frankie replied right away.

He also contacted the Esterhaszes.

I won't repeat what Shirley said. But Gord's dad and one of Gord's sisters want to sit down with Jacob.

Will this trip help Jacob? I have no idea. Everything – including us – is unclear. But that's life, I guess. We know we can't do a rewrite. We can't undo what's been done, or control what's coming next.

All we can do is hope for the best.

I'm trying to be optimistic.

ACKNOWLEDGEMENTS

Heaps of gratitude to:

The experts in their fields for being so generous with their time, and for helping me to not look foolish: my friend Gordon Kopelow, a great lawyer who always graciously takes the time to answer my questions, all for the cost of a diner lunch; lawyer and best-selling author Robert Rotenberg for taking time out of his busy schedule to answer my questions about Ontario law (and my dear friend Moira Holmes for the introduction); Brian Montague and Randy Fincham of the Vancouver Police Department, who are always so fast to respond to my 'yes but what would happen if...?' questions; and to Catherine MacMillan, for being a far better counsellor than any of the ones in this book (with the exception of the one who appears at the end, who will become as good as Catherine, I am sure of it).

Susan Juby, Linda Bailey and Ross King for reading the manuscript at various stages and giving me such thoughtful and considered notes. I am in awe of your writing talent and delighted to count you all as friends. Susan Juby, IOU one title, since you inadvertently gave me mine.

My husband Goran Fernlund, for reading – and re-reading – and re-reading – the manuscript, for making sure my bionic arm stuff was accurate, and for letting me talk about it on long walks after dinner.

Wendy Russell, TV personality and crafter extraordinaire, for letting me put the real, live you in my book.

Hilary McMahon, for always being a voice of honesty and reason when I need it most, and for just being so good at your job.

All the folks at Tundra, Wendy Lamb Books and Andersen Press, some of whom I've met face to face, some of whom I've only met via email: Dana Carey, Colleen Fellingham, Peter Phillips, Pamela Osti, Aisha Cloud, Sarah Kimmelman, Chloe Sackur, Harriet Dunlea and everyone else – for all the hard work you do.

My editors. I feel like I won the lottery, getting to work with Tara Walker, Wendy Lamb and Charlie Sheppard – in this case three is definitely not a crowd. Your notes, patience, kindness and nurturing through the growing pains of this novel – well, I mean it when I say I could not have done it without you. My gratitude is infinite.

Lastly, to the internet, that great time-suck, for all the info I ever needed on cool crafts and freak deaths – but especially for all the awesome cat videos.

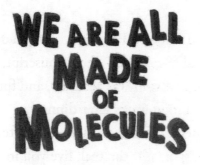

WE ARE ALL MADE OF MOLECULES

A NOVEL BY SUSIN NIELSEN

Longlisted for the Carnegie Medal

Stewart is geeky, gifted but socially clueless. His mom has died and he misses her every day. Ashley is popular, cool but her grades stink. Her dad has come out and moved out – but not far enough.

Their worlds are about to collide: Stewart and his dad are moving in with Ashley and her mom. Stewart is 89.9% happy about it even as he struggles to fit in at his new school. But Ashley is 110% horrified and can't get used to her totally awkward home. And things are about to get a whole lot more mixed up when they attract the wrong kind of attention. . .

'Snappy and witty. A really fine YA novel' *Telegraph*

'I defy you not to fall in love with this book' *Phil Earle*

9781783443765   £7.99